MISBEHAVING

Wanted: Adventurous, open-minded man willing to try anything...

As a popular sex blogger, Beatriz gets paid to have orgasms. So being on deadline the week of her sister's wedding isn't as rough as it sounds. There's just one hitch: Bea's assignment is to write a review of a sex position manual, but she doesn't have a plus one to play with.

THE GOOD NEWS: Ben, the one who got away back in college, is also attending stag—and he's as temptingly gorgeous as ever.

THE BAD NEWS: Ben turned down Bea's offer of graduation-night sex five years ago.

THE BEST NEWS: He's not planning on making the same mistake twice.

A red-hot retelling of *Much Ado About Nothing* for people who love Shakespeare but thought his plays could use a few more sex scenes.

MISBEHAVING

TIFFANY REISZ

8TH CIRCLE PRESS • LOUISVILLE, KY

With apologies to the Bard...

CHAPTER ONE

Something vibrated in Beatriz's bed. This wasn't an unusual occurrence, except that when vibrating happened in her bed, Beatriz was usually in the bed. She heard the buzzing from her bathroom and sighed.

"Don't be John," she said as she raced from the bathroom to the bed and started digging through her sheets. "I don't have time for you today..."

She found her phone and glared at the screen.

"*Me estás jodiendo?*" she swore when she saw the name "JOHN THE BASTARD" pop up on her screen. With a sigh she took the call, knowing he'd keep calling until she answered. "John, I turned in everything three days ago."

"I know, I know," he said, sounding un-characteristically apologetic. "But I need you."

"I don't like hearing those words from any man I'm not sleeping with."

"Are you hitting on me, Bea?"

Beatriz sighed heavily into the phone and hoped it created ear-splitting feedback on the other end of the line. "My Uber is on its way right now," she said. "I'm spending a week in Essex for my sister's wedding. I don't have time for this."

"Not my problem," he said, sounding like the good old John the Bastard she knew. "Angie just called. Her column's going to be late."

"New boyfriend?"

"Medical crisis, Bea. Have some sympathy."

"What's her problem?"

"Carpal tunnel, from too much mas-turbating."

"Occupational hazard. I have no sympathy."

"Bea, behave."

"You're glitching, John."

"Look, I'll leave you alone. But I need a thousand words from you this week to fill Angie's slot."

"As much as I'd love to fill Angie's slot, I'm a little busy this week doing wedding stuff with my family. Remember when I emailed you six months ago and said, 'Leave me alone the last week in August because my only sister is getting married'?"

"Nope."

"Well, I did. Family wedding time is not really the best time to be trying out new sex toys, okay?"

"I wouldn't ask if it wasn't an emergency. And you don't have to try out new toys. You can do a book review."

Beatriz sighed. "A book review? I don't get orgasms doing book reviews."

"You have to write something for me, Bea."

"Fine. As long as Angie promises to return the favor sometime."

"Does this mean you'll have at least a thousand words for me in my inbox by Sunday night?"

"Sometimes I think I'm kinky because of how often I fantasize about slapping you. Then I realize I just really want to slap you."

"Beatriz," John said in a stern voice. "Pause and take one little moment to re-member that I pay you four hundred dollars a month to review sex toys. In other words, I pay you to have orgasms. Are you thinking about that?"

Beatriz paused, took a moment and remembered. "Okay, you have a point there. I'll get you a book review. I have a stack of unopened envelopes from publishers on my desk anyway."

"Good. Now give me your hotel address so I can send you this new box of stuff I want you to review by next Sunday."

"The slapping fantasy has returned."

Beatriz gave him the hotel information. Hotel Essex, Essex, New York, care of Claudia Spears—her sister, she reminded him, who was about to get married. As she finished giving him the address, her phone buzzed to alert her that her Uber had arrived and was waiting outside the front door of her brownstone.

"Gotta go. My ride is here."

"Have fun," John said.

"Have fun writing a book review?"

"You'll find a way to make it fun, Bea. You always do..."

Without another word Bea hung up on him and tossed the phone into her purse. She shouldered her bag, grabbed her suitcase, and raced past the desk in her tiny home office. A stack of unopened bubble mailers had been accumulating on her chair for weeks. The return address label on the top envelope read "Brown Paper Publishing." She knew Brown Paper. A boutique press, they specialized in coffee table books on risqué subject matter. Great. Perfect. Wonderful. Lots of pictures and very little text. Easy review for a busy Bea.

Beatriz shoved the envelope into her purse and headed out to her Uber. She threw her stuff in the backseat and confirmed her destination with the driver, the airport. Once they were on their way she pulled the envelope out of her purse. Maybe she could flip through the book on the plane ride upstate. She'd get the reading and the reviewing over with as soon as possible so she could relax and enjoy all the pre-wedding partying with her sister, Claudia, and Henry, her fiancé. This wouldn't be a problem. Not a problem at all.

With one tear she ripped the envelope open and pulled out the book. *THE MANUAL* it read in big gold type on a black cover. She flipped it over to the back and read the cover copy. *A Sex Position Manual for Millennials. If you read it, you will come...*

Sex position manual? Beatriz nearly groaned aloud. There was only one way to review a sex position manual and that was by having sex with someone. And here she was on her way to a wedding with no date, no boyfriend, and no time to go back to her apartment and get another book. Which meant only one thing.

Once she got to Essex, she would have to find someone to sleep with.

"Fuck," she breathed.

"Fuck what?" the driver repeated, a smile on her face.

"No," Beatriz said. "Fuck who."

That was the question.

Ben arrived at the Essex Hotel just in time to keep Henry from drinking himself into a stupor at the bar. The groom-to-be had two empty beer bottles and one full shot glass in front of him. Henry reached for the shot and Ben covered it with his hand.

"Hey, whoa," Henry said. "No shot-blocking."

"I'm here to save you from yourself." Ben slapped him on the back as he removed the shot glass from Henry's vicinity. "Friends don't let friends drink and wed."

Henry groaned and leaned back in his bar stool before seemingly discovering there was no back to a bar stool. Ben grabbed his shoulder to steady him.

"Thank you." Henry lifted his empty beer

bottle in a salute. "Sit. Talk. Keep me from drinking. Drinking more, I mean."

"Why are you drinking, anyway?" Ben took the stool next to him. A pretty bartender, dark skin and ebony eyes, gave him a broad smile and an "I'll be right there" wink as she poured a glass of wine for another customer. "Aren't you happy? Big day coming up? Marriage? Kids? The dream all men dream of?"

Henry glared at Ben and Ben laughed.

"I hate you," Henry said. "And I hate you for the following three reasons. Number one—you've been here two minutes and the bartender is already flirting with you."

"I can't help that I'm prettier than you."

"Number two." Henry held up two fingers and feigned shoving them in Ben's eyes. "I love Claudia. I can't wait to marry her. But if she ever makes me have a wedding again, I'm going to divorce her. Well, just her family. She can stay."

"Future mother-in-law driving you batshit?" Ben asked.

"Yes. Very batshit. But the wedding planner's worse. Wants me to ask my own brother to step down as best man. Something about height symmetry."

"Next time you get married...don't."

Henry tapped his forehead. "Genius, you are."

"Thank you. I think I get smarter with every breakup."

"You must be Einstein by now. Are you going to date and dump the bartender this week? She's giving you the eyes." Henry looked at the bartender and back at Ben.

"She does have nice eyes," Ben agreed and then put all thoughts of beautiful bartenders out of his mind. "But no. After Katie, I swore off women for a year. I just need a break."

"No women for a year? You?" Henry scoffed. "I give it two days."

"It's already been two months. And what's the third reason?" Ben asked.

"The what?"

"The third reason you hate me, you half-drunk asshole."

"Oh. Because you took my drink away, you not-drunk asshole."

"Mine," Ben said and downed the shot. He didn't drink much, not anymore. Unavoidable adulthood had forced him to do terrible, awful things like drink less, eat better, and work out more often. He'd never felt younger, healthier or more energetic since he started acting his age. How depressing. "If it makes you feel any better, man, I hate you, too."

Henry nodded. "Yeah, I don't blame you for that."

"You do know why Katie dumped me, right?" Ben asked. Henry gave him a guilty look.

"Does it start with a B?"

"She caught me reading Beatriz's blog."

"Reading it or, you know, *reading* it?"

"What do you think? When I told her who she was..." Ben winced at the memory of his final fight with Katie. The relationship would never have worked anyway. Katie wanted marriage and kids and as soon as possible. He needed more time to focus on his career and figure out what he wanted from life before going down that path of no return. And then she'd caught him masturbating to a blog column written by the one woman he'd never gotten over...

"Don't kill me or anything, dude," Henry said. "But speaking of people whose names start with B..."

"What?" Ben asked the question slowly, emphasizing every single letter in the word.

"You're going to need to get back in drinking shape by tomorrow."

Ben narrowed his eyes at Henry. "Why?" He drew the "why" out as long as possible to maximize the threatening tone in his voice.

"Because...well, Bea's coming."

"What? I thought she was in Spain."

"She was. But she moved back to the States two months ago. Just in time to come to the wedding."

"You have got to be shitting me." Ben's stomach dropped. Then it jumped back up at the thought of seeing Beatriz for the first time since college. Would she look the same? Leggy, brown-haired, dark-eyed and beautiful? Talk the same? Sexy Spanish accent and nine kinds of attitude? Smell the same? Vanilla and strawberry shampoo?

"Ben, she's Claudia's foster sister. She's in the wedding. You both are in the wedding. So, you know, take that."

Ben took it. He took it hard. Beatriz... He'd loved that woman in college. He could own that now. Back then he'd pretended Beatriz was just another girl he wanted to sleep with, and when he'd missed his shot, he told himself it was no big loss. But here he was, five years later, still thinking about her.

"Is she here yet?" Ben asked.

Henry raised an eyebrow at him and Ben's

stomach dropped once more. It went down and stayed down this time. Ben watched as Henry spun around in his bar stool and pointed across the lobby. He followed Henry's gaze to where it stopped on a woman, tall with long, straight black hair and deep copper skin. She had on jeans, a camisole that did nothing to disguise the fullness of her breasts, and a wide grin on her face as she chatted with the man at the registration desk. She was, in fact, the most beautiful woman in the entire world.

"She's here now," Henry said.

Ben stared at Beatriz across the lobby. She didn't see him, thank God, so he could stare all he wanted.

"Orange," Ben said, noting the color of Beatriz's shirt. "She's wearing an orange shirt and orange high heels."

"So?"

"She's the only woman I've ever known who wears orange. She looks like a tropical flower, doesn't she? God, she looks good in orange."

"Man, I thought I was the drunk one."

Ben looked down at the empty shot glass and back up at the bartender. She waited for his order. Five minutes ago she'd been a gorgeous woman he'd had fun flirting with. Now she was only the bartender. Good thing. What he needed right now was a bartender and nothing else. He pointed at the shot glass. She refilled it and started to walk off.

"Wait," he said to her. She turned around with that same seductive smile. A smile that disappeared after his next three words. "Leave the bottle."

CHAPTER THREE

Beatriz checked into the hotel at nine that evening, *THE MANUAL* still burning a hole in her bag. While the man at the desk processed her credit card and paperwork, Beatriz scanned the lobby, looking for any suitable candidates to help her with her review. Maybe she'd get lucky and an "Attractive Men Looking For No Strings Attached Sexual Intercourse" conference would be happening at the Hotel Essex this week. She saw a few teenage boys loitering by the fountain. Too young. Three older couples talked in the vestibule. Too couple-y. A pretty woman about her age strode through the lobby pulling a wheeled suitcase behind her. Too female. Most of the time she wouldn't have any problem with a few nights in bed with another woman, but the sex position manual was for heterosexual couples. Plus women tended to get clingy. She had no time for clingy.

She heard a shriek from the elevator area and Beatriz took a steadying breath. Speaking of clingy women...

"Oh, my God!" Claudia rushed toward her and wrapped her up in a bear hug. Beatriz hugged back, knowing that when caught in a Claudia-hug, much like quicksand, the harder a person struggled, the more trapped he or she became. Best to simply relax and take it. This, incidentally, was her philosophy for anal sex, as well. "When did you get in?"

"Just now. Checking in. You look amazing." Beatriz pulled back enough to give Claudia a once-over. She hadn't seen her foster sister in over a year. She'd expected her to look haggard from wedding planning, but she wore the look of love. "Engaged looks good on you. Where's Henry?"

"Hiding in the bar," Claudia said while the bellhop put Beatriz's bags on the luggage rack. "The wedding planner's driving him nuts. I'm about ready to hit her myself. Got any connections?"

"I do," said the bellhop.

Beatriz made a mental note to give the bellhop a good tip.

"How bad is it?" she asked Claudia.

"Long story. It involves her trying to get Henry to rearrange his groomsmen so they line up by height. She thinks the tallest one should be his best man. Henry's brother was not amused."

"Short men deserve love, too. Is Mark still single?"

Claudia shook her head. "Nope. He's here with his girlfriend. Why?"

"I need to get laid. It's work-related."

Claudia nodded. She knew all about Beatriz's work.

"I have connections there, too," said the bellhop. *KEATON*, his name tag indicated.

"I love this guy," Beatriz said as they neared the elevators.

"So what's the job?" Claudia asked as the three of them got on the first elevator.

"I have a book to review by Monday. Sex position manual creatively entitled *THE MANUAL*. They call it '*The Joy of Sex* for Millennials!' Complete with exclamation point."

"What's a Millennial?"

"Us."

"Got it. We'll find someone to do you. Some Millennial."

"I like older men. Gen X works, too."

"A couple of the groomsmen are single," Claudia said. "Jake's here."

"No way. He always wears too much body spray. I'd need a hazmat suit. Hazmat suits are not sexy."

"Speak for yourself," Keaton the bellhop muttered.

"Jed?" Claudia suggested.

"We hooked up in college. He's terrible in bed."

"Really?" Claudia sounded stunned. "He seems so confident. Cocky, even."

"It's a cover. Guilt. Momma complex. You have sex and then fifteen minutes later he's giving you the 'I don't think we should do this anymore' routine. I told him his cock wasn't worth cutting through all the red tape for."

"You go, girl." Keaton nodded his approval as the elevator door opened.

The three of them disembarked and headed for room 424.

"Well...there is one other option," Claudia said as they reached Beatriz's hotel room.

"Not worry about it since you're getting married in five days?" Beatriz asked.

"Not that. Getting you laid is much more fun than getting me married." Claudia helped Keaton with the bags.

"Then what?" Beatriz asked.

Claudia smiled at her. It wasn't a good smile. It was a "don't kill me" smile. Immediately Beatriz thought of a plethora of ways to kill Claudia.

"Ben's here, isn't he?"

Claudia winced. "Sort of. He's one of the groomsmen."

"You told me he wasn't coming," Beatriz almost shouted.

"He wasn't coming, because of a work thing. Then he got a promotion. So now he is coming. I mean, he came."

"So Ben's here?" Beatriz glared at Claudia.

"Ben's here."

"Right now?"

"Right now."

"Who's Ben?" Keaton asked, leaning against the luggage rack and smiling.

"My ex-nothing," Beatriz said.

"She was in love with him in college, but nothing ever came of it. She's still a little bitter."

"I'm not bitter. I'm just still mildly disappointed in him. You know, as a human being. Because he never fucked me, and he should have."

"Yes, he should've," Keaton said.

"Thank you. I owe you money, right?" Beatriz asked.

"I wouldn't want to impose." Keaton waggled his eyebrows.

Beatriz handed him a five-dollar bill. He gave Lincoln a quick kiss and headed for the door with the luggage rack.

"You should leave the rack," Claudia said. "She's having crazy sex this week with someone she doesn't know yet. She may need that."

"If she needs it back, call the front desk," Keaton said as he pulled the luggage rack out of the room. "Put the wheel brake on first. Voice of experience."

Alone now in the room with Claudia, Beatriz started to unpack.

"I can't believe you didn't tell me Ben's here," Beatriz said, angrily removing her underwear from her suitcase.

"I didn't want you bailing on the wedding."

"I wouldn't bail on the wedding. But if I

knew he was going to be here, I would have mentally prepared myself to see him again."

"Mentally prepared as in...?"

"I would have brought a date with me. I have a male escort who owes me. Although I think one of the Real Housewives has him booked this weekend."

"Your life is weird, Bea."

"What? Because I'm a sex education blogger?"

"For starters. Are you mad at me?"

"No, I'm not mad. He's one of Henry's best friends so of course he's here. He should be here." Beatriz hung her dresses up in the closet and started sorting through her shoes. "I just don't want things to be weird."

"It shouldn't be. You haven't seen him since college."

"True, but we didn't part on the best of terms. The day he graduated I went to his room in a bathrobe, took it off and stood naked in front of him. I told him to fuck me like he'd never fucked anyone before. I knew I'd probably never see him again so why not? No strings attached. No pressure. Only beautiful sex. My graduation present to him."

"I never knew you and Ben had sex."

Beatriz's heart stuttered at the memory of

standing naked in front of Ben in his dorm room. He'd already packed everything up. Nothing remained but the bed, the sheets, him, and her. The way he'd looked at her when she dropped the robe, she knew she had him. Not only did he want her, he adored her. He drank up the sight of her like a man who'd walked across a desert and found his oasis. Or so she'd thought.

"We didn't. He said he was sorry, but he wasn't interested. He asked me to go." Beatriz would never forget the burning sting of humiliation. Her whole body had blushed at his rejection of her.

"What the hell? What straight man in his right mind says no to that offer?"

"Ben did. So I said something horrible to him, put on the robe and walked out. I cried all night. The next morning, I decided he was dead to me."

"Beatriz...why didn't you tell me this?"

"You were graduating, too. You had more important things on your mind. Plus, it was so humiliating. Not my finest moment."

Claudia sat on the bed and looked up at Beatriz, who tried looking at anything but her sister and the pity in her eyes.

"And here we are—it's just like college

again. You're with Henry, and I'm stewing over Ben." Beatriz sat on the other bed across from Claudia. "It's just, I loved him, you know? I didn't let myself love anyone else but him. And maybe that's for the best. But I spent an entire year trying to be with him, and he said he didn't want me. That's fine. No one is supposed to want me. But then why did he kiss me like he did that night we met? Why did he tell me he wanted me on a Thursday, but by Friday it was poof—gone?" She blew into her fingertips.

"I don't know. I thought he was crazy about you, too."

"He took me for a tour of campus. You remember that? My first week at Brooks? I told him I was born in El Salvador and only made it to the U.S. when I was ten. You know what he said?"

Claudia shook her head. The sadness in Beatriz's voice clutched at her throat.

"He said, '*Más vale tarde que nunca.*'"

"What does that mean?"

"Better late than never." Beatriz smiled. She'd been so impressed that Ben, this blue-eyed all-American boy, spoke Spanish, and spoke it so well. He hadn't asked her any questions about her past, about why she'd come to America, where her parents were. People did that, even total strangers, not realizing that if a ten-year-old girl had to leave her family and her country behind, then it was probably not the sort of story you'd tell to someone you just met. No. Ben said, "Better late than never," as if he was the reason she'd ended up in this country. And at that moment she'd believed that he was.

"I know you loved him. I remember." Claudia sat on the bed next to her. "Your freshman year was rough. It broke my heart watching him break your heart."

"It was like I had two hearts and both of them were in love with him. I never knew you could feel that much. And he just had the one heart and it wasn't interested in me."

"I thought for sure he'd come around about you. I'd never seen two people more perfect together than you two. Not even me and Henry."

"In college, Henry wore his underwear on the outside of his pants."

"Now you know why it took him five years to convince me to marry him." Claudia winked at Beatriz who leaned against her sister and kissed her on the cheek.

"I'm very happy you're getting married to Henry," Beatriz said.

"I am, too. Now we just have to find you someone to be happy with."

"I am happy, I promise. Spain was amazing, but it's great to be back in the States again. Great to be here with you." She smiled at her sister, a bright, genuine smile that she hoped convinced Claudia not to worry about her. She was so happy for Claudia and Henry. They belonged together. And Claudia needed to focus on her own wedding and not her foster sister's five-year-old heartbreak.

"You'll be okay?" Claudia asked, squeezing Beatriz's shoulder.

"Totally okay. Promise. Or I will be as soon as I find someone to have sex with this week," Beatriz said.

"God, it really is like being back in college."

Claudia slammed the hotel door behind her and raced to the bed. Henry groaned as she threw herself on top of him.

"Easy, babe. I had too much to drink."

"Two beers?" she asked, planting kisses along his jawline.

"And a half."

"You're such a lightweight." She threw her leg over his stomach and he caressed her thigh. "I love you anyway, even if you do have the drinking prowess of a ten-year-old girl."

"Hey, I've known some hard-drinking ten-year-olds."

"Liar. Kiss me, I'm horny."

"Best four words ever spoken." He kissed her on the mouth and rolled her onto her back. "Thought you'd be too tired tonight."

"Never too tired for you inside me." She grinned up at him. Her newly manicured hands slid through his dark blond hair. A ravenous twinkle shone in his eyes.

"Dirty talk from my angelic bride? Someone's been talking to Bea."

"She just puts me in the mood. I think she's like a sex goddess. You get near her and you want to have sex with anything that moves."

"Anything that moves?"

"Or anything stationary. I don't want to limit my options."

"How's Miss Bea-havior doing?" Henry asked as he slid his hand under Claudia's shirt. He cupped her breast lightly and caressed her hardening nipple with his thumb.

"Miss Bea-having, as usual. She brought her work with her this week."

"Oh, damn. Did she have the bellhop cart up ten boxes of dildos and vibrators?"

"Worse. She has to review a sex position manual. She's on the hunt for a fuck buddy."

Henry unhooked her bra. "Well, I'd volunteer, but I'm too busy being your fuck buddy."

"What do you think about Ben?"

"I could be his fuck buddy."

"I mean for Bea. I still think they'd make a great couple."

Henry groaned and rolled onto his back.

"Hey, no. Hand back on the boob," she said, grabbing Henry's hand and putting it back where it belonged.

"Sorry," he said, moving her bra out of the way and pressing his hand to her bare breast. She sighed with pleasure. "But Ben's still got it for her, I think. At least he's still pissed at himself for not going after her when he had the chance. It could get ugly and weird if those two get together."

"Or sexy and awesome. Why not? What happened with them anyway? Did Ben ever tell you why he flaked out on her? Because I swear it was love and lust at first sight when we introduced them."

Claudia remembered that night. She'd been relieved Beatriz had decided to follow her to Brooks College. Beatriz had battled some problems in high school and at least Claudia could keep an eye on her baby foster sister for her first year of college. Newly single Ben had shown up at her dorm room looking for Henry. Beatriz saw Ben. Ben saw Beatriz. Claudia had laughed out loud as her feisty, fearless sister turned the full force of her considerable charm on Ben. Poor gorgeous Ben, who owned any room he walked into, had turned tongue-tied as Beatriz interrogated him. Did he like Brooks? Yes, he loved it here but couldn't wait to graduate. What was his major? Business administration. What did he plan to do with a business administration degree? Administrate businesses, maybe? Would his work help or hinder the progress of the human race and specifically the rights of women in underdeveloped countries? Um…yes?

Claudia had to cover her mouth with her hand to hide her smile that night. She'd wished she'd had some popcorn to watch the Beatriz and Ben Show. Beatriz had found Ben's answers entirely acceptable and had proceeded to ask him to show her around campus. Such a simple request and yet Ben had smiled as if he'd won the lottery. As they walked out the door together, Claudia had told herself that those two would be engaged by graduation. She knew it in her heart. Well, her heart was wrong.

She looked at Henry across the pillows and saw he wore a guilty look on his face.

"What?" she asked. "What's wrong?"

"Nothing."

"Your hand is no longer on my boob and you look like you just killed someone. I don't really care if you killed someone, so long as you get back to the boob job."

"I didn't kill anybody."

"That's good."

"But I did sort of do something bad."

Claudia sat up and looked down at Henry. He sat up as well and leaned back against the headboard.

"What did you do?" she asked.

Henry winced. "Don't call off the wedding, okay? I did it for us."

"Tell me. Tell me right now."

"I was in love with you. Crazy in love with you. And I wanted you to be in love with me, too, just as much. Then when Ben met Bea, and he told me he had fallen hard and fast for my girlfriend's baby sister, I saw the end of the world. So I kind of asked him not to pursue her."

"You *what?*" Claudia nearly yelled the words at him. She picked up the pillow, ready to hit him with it the moment another stupid confession came out of his mouth.

"She was a freshman. Barely eighteen. And Ben was almost twenty-three. And he'd had ten girlfriends in the last two years. Ten,

Claudia. Ten." Henry held up two hands and wiggled all ten fingers. "My best friend dumping your baby sister? Not good. The opposite of good. Bad, even. When Ben told me he'd met the girl of his dreams, I saw the apocalypse."

"The apocalypse?"

"The SEXpocalypse. Ben already had a job offer on the West Coast. Did you really want him having sex with her all year and then dumping her the day he graduated?"

"Well...not really," Claudia admitted.

"And Ben was an old senior. You know he was twenty-three and she was eighteen? You remember that part?"

"I sort of forgot that part."

"You would have hated Ben for dumping Bea and then hated me because he was my best friend. I couldn't face that. I told him you wouldn't want him dating your sister because of the age difference. So he did what I asked and backed off."

"Yeah, but he didn't. Because I was with you and she was with me, they were together for the entire school year. And she was in love with him and he wouldn't even give her the time of day. He treated her like his own baby sister."

"Yeah, he was nice and respectful and didn't once hit on her."

"She hated it."

"Do you hate me?"

"Yes." Claudia slammed the pillow down onto his stomach. He laughed and pulled her into his arms.

"I'm sorry, babe. I really didn't think that maybe they were actually in love with each other. Ben didn't want anything serious. That wasn't his style. I thought they just wanted to fuck, and they could do that with anybody."

"True," Claudia said. Beatriz had a gift for wrapping guys around her finger and Ben had a line of young ladies waiting to be his next one-night to two-week stand.

"You were the only person in the world to me back then. I would have done anything to keep us together. Forgive me? My cock and my heart were in the right place, right?" Henry asked, putting on his puppy dog eyes.

"I forgive you. Maybe." Claudia could never resist the puppy dog eyes. "I mean, you're probably right. He probably would have dumped her. He's had as many girlfriends as Bea's had boyfriends and that's saying something," Claudia agreed somewhat reluctantly. She sort of liked painting Ben and

Henry as the bad guys. She hated to admit that Henry had a point.

"Ben was seriously stoked about the job waiting for him after graduation. He couldn't wait to get his ass out of Brooks. I think Ben would have crushed her if they'd gotten together back then."

"Probably."

"See? I knew I was right. I'm the hero here, really." Henry puffed his chest out. Claudia rolled her eyes.

"Being right doesn't make it okay."

"How do I make it okay?" Henry asked. "I love Ben and I love Bea, and I really want you to take all your clothes off. And I'll do whatever it takes to get you naked. And make them happy. But mostly get you naked."

Claudia sighed. "We have to fix this. She's still mad at him. He's still mad at you. That means...they aren't over each other."

"Good point. So what now?"

Claudia knelt on the bed and pulled her shirt off. "Well, Bea has this book review to write. She's gotta find a partner to have sex with since the book is a sex position manual for Millennials."

"What's a Millennial?" Henry asked.

"Us."

"Gotcha."

"You see, Bea has to try out the positions in the book. What if we tell Ben that Bea wants him to be her book buddy?"

"And tell Bea what?" Henry asked.

"We'll tell Bea that Ben volunteered to help her out with this book thing. And so he'll go to her room expecting sex. She'll open the door expecting sex. They'll have sex. And either it'll work or it won't and it doesn't matter either way because you and I are getting married no matter what." Claudia pulled off her bra and started to shimmy out of her jeans.

"Worth a shot. Anything to get me out of the doghouse and into doggie style."

"Good. Go talk to Ben."

"Can I fuck my bride-to-be first, please?"

"No. Ben first. Then me."

"I have to fuck Ben first? Good thing he's pretty. You know he was bisexual for one week in college?"

"Henry."

"And you can just get lost in those blue eyes. I call that color Chris Pine blue."

"Henry."

"I want to be the Spock to his Kirk. You know, the J.J. Abrams reboot, not the original series."

"Henry!" Claudia flicked his nose—hard.

"I'm going. I'm going. Don't start without me."

Claudia tossed her panties at Henry's back as he headed to the door. As soon as he was gone, she picked up the phone and called Bea's room.

"Bea's answering machine," came the voice over the line. "Please leave a message at the beep."

"This is the Hotel Essex," Claudia said, rolling her eyes. "And no one has owned an answering machine in twenty years. And you're just trying to annoy me."

"Beep," Beatriz said.

"Hi Bea, it's Claudia," Claudia began. Bea often faked her own answering machine, especially when she knew who was calling, for the sole purpose of annoying them. That's okay. Claudia knew exactly how to get her revenge. "I just wanted you to know that Ben was into you during college, and he still is. Henry asked him not to pursue you because of me. That's all. No need to call me back. Bye. Oh, and if you ask him to have sex with you this week so you can work on your book report thingie, he probably would go for it."

Claudia hung up the phone. Immediately

her hotel phone rang. She didn't answer it. She heard a buzzing from her purse—Beatriz calling her cell. She ignored that call as well.

Five minutes and fifteen unanswered phone calls later, Henry walked back in the room. Claudia lay naked on the bed. She rose up on her elbows and looked at him with a cocked eyebrow.

"So?" she asked.

"He's on his way to her room right now."

"Good," Claudia said. "Now we can have sex."

CHAPTER FIVE

Ben stared at the door to Beatriz's hotel room. She was there, behind that door. Right there. The last time he'd seen her she'd been completely naked and standing in his dorm room. That was five years ago. So much had happened since then. He'd gotten his first real job working for Google, gotten promoted, and almost gotten engaged. This could have been his wedding weekend, but thankfully he realized his girlfriend wasn't in love with *him*, only with the idea of being married. Neither of them cried over the breakup. A good sign that breaking up was the right thing to do. He'd moved three times since college and changed jobs twice, but during all that he'd held on to one constant: Beatriz.

She probably didn't know he read the

Miss Bea Haven column she wrote for *The Daily Cocktail*. He'd messaged Claudia on Facebook last year and asked, as casually as he could, what Beatriz was up to.

Living in Spain, Claudia had said. Beatriz had a great job working as a translator for a European publisher. *She also writes a column for a big website that acts as the repository of all things sex on the internet. Beatriz reviews sex toys and sex books. Nice work if you can get it,* Claudia joked.

Hearing that, Ben had broken the internet record for fastest-ever Google search. He found Beatriz's column and read every single post Beatriz had written. He hadn't read them all at once. He had to take a break—or two or three—between articles. "Miss Bea Haven" wrote in detail about her experiences with different types of vibrators—what worked for her, what didn't, how she used them, how they made her feel. He could just see that beautiful woman lying naked on her bed pleasuring herself for hours on end. Who needed porn when he had these sex toy reviews? Knowing Beatriz, she'd stop every few minutes to take notes —vibrator in one hand, notepad in the other.

Ben even had whole sentences from her reviews memorized. He hadn't tried to memorize them. He wasn't that much of a desperate, horny stalker. But certain sentences had burned themselves into his mind.

The Lady Angel vibrator was a comfortable fit for a woman who enjoys deep penetration and a wide shaft as much as I do.

The orgasm the Black Prince produces makes your PC muscles buck like a stallion. My partner's tongue provided the clitoral stimulation. The resulting orgasm was a top ten moment.

The G-spot massager from the Sirena series should come with a warning—don't use on a day you actually need to get out of your bed. I had so much fun with it that I had ten orgasms in one day and had to change my sheets twice.

He'd never been so jealous of sex toys in his life.

What he wouldn't give to curl up in bed with Beatriz while she did her work, watching her come over and over again. He'd happily lend a helping hand. Or two. And once she came she would be so wet he could slide right inside her and stay there all day and all night long.

"Down, boy," Ben said to his erection. He took a few deep breaths to calm himself. He still couldn't believe he was doing this, standing outside Bea's door. But Henry had been annoyingly insistent.

"Dude, I told Claudia that I told you back in college not to pursue Bea because of, you know, reasons. Mainly me being a pussy. Claudia hit me with a pillow and she won't let me have sex with her until I tell you that I was wrong about doing that. So...sorry. You should probably go talk to Bea. She still likes you or something. I can't remember exactly what Claudia said. I had trouble hearing over my hard-on."

Ben wanted to believe Henry. Only one way to find out. Ben didn't let Henry finish talking before he'd stalked past him and into the hallway. When he made it halfway down the hall he turned around.

Henry stood by his room, smiling at him.

"What's her room number?" Ben had asked.

"It's 424. Go. Have all the fun. Make all the love. You're welcome."

He couldn't believe Beatriz still wanted

him after all this time. After all, he knew he'd hurt and humiliated her the last time they saw each other. He'd wanted her so badly that day he could barely breathe when he remembered seeing her beautiful naked body for the first and last time. High, full breasts, long, toned legs, hips he wanted to dig his fingers into when he buried his face between her thighs. Telling her no had nearly killed him. Only Henry's pleading that he leave Claudia's little sister alone, and his preemptive guilt over having sex with someone and then moving to the West Coast the very next day, kept him from taking her up on every single little thing she offered.

Maybe now he could make up for lost time.

But should he?

He stared at the door to room 424. She still lived on the opposite coast from him. They hadn't seen each other since he graduated college. They were here to support Claudia and Henry for their wedding, not rehash all their old drama.

But then again...they might end up naked.

Didn't matter. He wasn't here to have sex with her. He was here to talk. Just talk. They should talk. While talking, he would tell her that while he was an idiot for letting Henry talk him out of pursuing her in college, the truth was he'd been terrified he'd end up just like Henry if he hadn't backed away from her. Henry had been head-over-heels in love with Claudia. Even back in college Henry had been ready to give up everyone and everything to make his girlfriend happy. And Ben didn't have the luxury of falling in love and throwing caution to the wind. He'd been the first person in his family to go to college, to get a degree and an offer of a high-paying job. He couldn't let them down by allowing his heart to steal his ambition.

"Wait," Ben muttered to the door. "Why am I saying this in my head and not to her?"

Ben pounded on her door.

Four agonizing seconds later, Beatriz opened the door. She wore a black silk bathrobe and looked at him in total shock as if she'd been expecting anyone but him at her door.

He looked at her. God, she'd only gotten more beautiful since college. She said nothing at all as she continued to stare at him. Rarely did anything shock Beatriz enough to silence her.

One of them had to say something, right?

He was the man. It should be him. He'd say the perfect thing. Something suave, something charming, something endearing that would make up for the last time they saw each other.

Ben opened his mouth to say he was sorry, to say he should have stood up to Henry and gone after what he wanted and given love a chance instead of bowing to his ambition and leaving her behind. He was going to say he should have slept with her when she offered, or at least given her a damn good reason why he hadn't.

"Will you have sex with me?" Beatriz asked.

Ben opened his mouth, then closed it again. Then opened it again. "Good to see you again, too, Bea."

Beatriz laughed and gave him an apologetic smile. "Sorry," she said, holding the door to her hotel room open, but not quite letting him inside yet. "One-track mind. I have to write an emergency book review on a sex position manual. I need a partner."

"A partner?"

"Well, you can't review a sex position manual without having sex, right?"

"Good point. Very good point," Ben said.

"So you want to...with me...review your book?"

"If you want to," she said, and smiled. That smile hit him right where it counted.

"You don't think we should talk first?"

"Talk about what?" she asked. "This is just for work, you know."

"Oh." Ben nodded. "Work."

"Think about it," she said, letting him in the room. The Hotel Essex was one of the more luxurious hotels he'd ever stayed in. Scarlet walls, black polished floors, elegant white rugs—it was an art deco dream come true. And in the middle of every room a huge king-size bed heaped in plush white linens beckoned. The headboards looked like thrones. The walls were decorated with real art, not hotel "art." And with the black-and-red-striped curtains pulled back and the moonlight shining, one could see the rolling hills blanketed with deep soft grass and lush leafy trees for miles. It was a far cry from a cramped dorm room.

"So how have you been?" she asked.

"Good. Great. I love my job. I guess you really love your job."

"Both jobs," she said as she sat on the bed and tapped a few keys on her laptop. He saw her save and close a document. He must have interrupted her at work. Surreptitiously he glanced around for any sex toys. Maybe she'd put them away before opening the door. "The blog work is the most fun, though. I guess Claudia told you what I'm doing?"

"Yeah, sex education blogger? Something like that?" He tried to sound nonchalant.

"Exactly like that. My boss is in a bind. He needs a thousand words by Sunday night. I thought I was reviewing a coffee table book. Wrong." She held up the book. It said *THE MANUAL* on the front in big gold letters.

"Sexy font," he said.

"Sexy book."

"Look...Bea," Ben said and sat on the end of her bed. "I wanted to tell you I was sorry. You know, about not having sex with you in college."

"That's what you're sorry about?"

"For starters," he said. "Henry asked me not to go after you because he was worried I'd dump you and Claudia would kill him over it."

"I like that my personal life was decided by you and Henry instead of me."

Ben winced. "Yeah...add that to the list of things I'm apologizing for."

"Well, I did sort of give you hell over it,

right?" Beatriz asked, a wicked gleam in her eyes.

"I think your last words to me were 'You fail as a man,'" Ben said. He remembered those words as if she'd spoken them yesterday. They'd burned themselves into his brain and he swore there and then he'd never fail as a man again.

Now it was Beatriz's turn to wince. "I said that?"

"You said that."

"Well, I was naked, offering you every square inch of my body inside and out, and you turned me down."

"I prefer to think of it as a supremely heroic act of self-sacrifice on my part. My best friend had never had a real girlfriend before Claudia and worried constantly he'd screw it up with this woman that he had declared was his 'soul mate' the day he met her."

"Soul mate?"

"He's more romantic than you'd expect for a guy who used to wear his underwear outside his pants."

"Smarter, too, if he loved Claudia that much from the beginning."

"Yeah, he's a good guy. The best guy. Hard to tell the guy who's been your best friend throughout your entire college career 'no' to a simple request not to fuck his girlfriend's baby sister."

"I get it. I do. It's for the best. You probably would have fucked me and forgotten me like Henry thought." Beatriz grinned at him, a smile that said, "I'm just giving you a hard time."

"But I didn't fuck you, and I've never forgotten you."

Beatriz's smile wavered a moment before returning full force. The combination of her bright white smile and her dark copper skin nearly blinded him. He wanted to see that smile a billion more times before the day he died. At least a billion.

"So...what are we doing here?" Ben asked. Beatriz closed her laptop and moved it to the bedside table.

"Getting reacquainted," she said. "And having sex if you're game. I'm sort of on deadline here."

"You're serious?"

Beatriz nodded. "As a heart attack. It's no-strings-attached sex. I won't even make you buy me flowers after. Think about it while I'm in the bathroom."

She left him sitting alone on the end of her bed while she went to the bathroom.

Ben took a deep breath and released it slowly. Think about it, she'd said. What was there to think about? Sex with the most beautiful woman in the world? Yes, please. Then again... this was work, she'd said. Just work. Nothing more than work. Did he want to be work? Cock for hire? He'd sworn off women for an entire year, hadn't he? Then again, he'd sworn off them because he knew he needed to get over Beatriz before dating anyone else. How was he supposed to get over Beatriz if Beatriz was under him?

"To do Bea...or not to do Bea...?" Ben asked himself.

Beatriz came out of the bathroom and stood in front of him. Her bathrobe was open just enough that he could see the curve of her breasts.

Who was he kidding?

"Let's do this," Ben said.

Beatriz grinned.

"Good. Thank you," she said. "Let's talk about the book. It's called *THE MANUAL* and it's being billed as 'The Joy of Sex for Millennials.'"

"What's a Millennial?"

"Us."

"Got it."

"It's a 'hip' sex guide," she said, putting hip in air quotes. "Most sex position manuals use a lot of technical terminology—it's all penis, vagina, cunnilingus, fellatio. *THE MANUAL* uses the words we use—vadge, cock and dick, blow job, going down, et cetera. Chapter four is titled *Fingerbanging for Fun and Profit*. It makes sexploration more approachable."

"Approachable?"

"Do you want to try ligotage?"

Ben rubbed the back of his neck. "That sounds terrifying. Isn't that something kings did to subjects who pissed them off?"

"It just means bondage. Rope. Handcuffs. Nothing scary. See how word choice can change the way you view a sex act?"

"Oh, bondage. That's better. But I left my handcuffs at home."

"Too bad," she said and gave him a wink. That wink sent his temperature shooting up ten degrees. It wasn't the only thing shooting up. "But we'll stick to the basics this week. There are twenty-five positions in the book. We just need to try out about five of them to give a fair review."

"Five?" Ben tried to mask his disappointment. As turned on as he was he could have tried out five tonight alone.

"Maybe more if we have time. I know you're busy this week. I don't want to impose on your cock."

"Impose on it. Please."

"Should we get started?"

"I will literally, actually, in reality die if we don't."

Beatriz laughed. "I can't have your death on my hands."

She shrugged out of her robe so casually that at first didn't even realize she was completely naked underneath it. As she bent over to pull the covers on the bed back, Ben nearly fainted at the sight of her shapely bottom and the hint of vaginal lips peeking out between her legs. He was going to be inside her...soon. Not soon enough.

"Wow," he said as he stared at her body.

"Wow?"

"I mean, you have a tattoo. I didn't know that," Ben said.

She turned her back to him. "Oh, that's my bumblebee. Had him for a couple years," she said, pointing out the tattoo on the back of her left shoulder. "He's the mascot for the Miss Bea Haven column."

Ben started to say "I know," but then he remembered she didn't know he obsessively read her column. He wasn't sure if she'd find it flattering or creepy that at least once a week he'd read her articles and masturbate to the images they conjured in his mind. Seeing her naked right now in front of him live and in living color put all his fantasies to shame. He'd forgotten how beautiful she was. He'd never forget again.

Ben started to strip out of his suit. He'd left his suit jacket in his hotel room so he only had to remove his tie, Oxford shirt, belt, shoes, socks, pants and boxer briefs.

"Dammit, I hate clothes," he said as he yanked at his tie.

"I like them," Beatriz said as she came to stand in front of him. She pushed his hands aside and started unbuttoning his shirt for him. "You look good in grown-up clothes."

"I had a meeting this morning with the big bosses. I'm usually a jeans and T-shirt guy."

"I remember. I loved your jeans. Remember that pair with the big hole in the right knee?"

"My lucky jeans."

"Those were my favorite. I always wondered how far I could reach if I slipped my arm in that hole."

"You dreamed of fisting my pants?"

"More like spelunking." She pulled his shirt off and laid it over the back of an armchair. He watched her as she unbuckled his belt, unzipped his pants. She had the most perfect light brown nipples. He couldn't wait to get his mouth on them, his fingers. He raised a hand and gently cupped her right breast. She looked up at him.

"Is that not okay?" he asked. He pulled his hand away. She smiled again.

"Of course it's okay. We're about to have sex. But we should probably go over what the book says before we get started."

"Right. Sure. The book." That's why they were doing this. The book. The book and his penis. Those two reasons. The book, his penis, her vagina—three reasons really. The book, his penis, her vagina, her breasts, her face, her smile, her perfect ass, her laugh, her lips, her hands that were now taking his pants off... He lost count of how many reasons they were doing this. He decided "infinity" would cover them all. "Is kissing... Is that okay? Or is this just—"

"You're not a john and I'm not a prostitute. Yes, we can kiss if you want. We're not going to get very far if you don't have an erection. So feel free to do whatever sort of foreplay you like."

"I think we're going to be okay on erections."

"I can see that," she said as she pushed his boxer briefs down his legs and eyed him.

"Is it... Am I..." Ben took a breath.

"Ben, are you nervous?"

"No, of course not," he said as Beatriz walked back to the bed and picked up the book. He ripped his socks off and followed her. "I have sex all the time. I had sex...recently." By recently he meant a couple months ago. He'd had a single fling after he and Katie broke up. Nothing since, but only because he'd sworn off women for a year. "I'm a sex haver."

"I didn't think you were a virgin. I remember college."

He grinned. "I've just never had sex that someone's going to write about and publish. Kind of makes you self-conscious. You know, about things."

"Things?"

"Like my penis. I mean, cock. What word does the book use?"

"All of them. Your penis/cock/dick/staff of manhood is fantastic. Very good size and super sexy. It's not even inside me yet, and I give it five bees."

"I have a five-bee penis?"

Bea always rated her sex toys on a one-to-five-bees scale. The more bees the better.

"For aesthetics," she said. "We'll have to try it out to see how it works."

"It works. I promise, it works."

"Good. Let's start with chapter two. It goes through some modifications of missionary position. Sit. Read. I'll get the lube and condoms."

"Lube?"

"Yes, lube. I'm wet but a little extra wetness never hurts. We're going to have a lot of sex this week. I don't want either of us getting chafed."

"True, true. I lub lube. I mean, love." He sat down, opened *THE MANUAL* to the page Bea had marked with a pink Post-it note. *Modified Missionary OR This Ain't Your Grandma's Wedding Night,* it read. He sighed. "We may need to deduct a bee for the mention of my grandmother."

"Good point." Beatriz scribbled a note on a piece of paper that lay by the bed.

"You actually wrote that down?"

"Sure," she said. "This is a book for partners. It has to work for both partners. I thought it was cute, but you thought referring to your grandmother's sex life was..."

"Unnerving," he said.

Beatriz wrote the word down. He kept reading.

Missionary position gets its name from the fact that missionaries in foreign lands would instruct the natives that the only God-sanctioned position for sexual intercourse was with the woman on her back and the man facing her on top. No wonder missionaries were often slaughtered by the natives.

Ben chuckled. "Okay, I'm giving it the bee back."

"Keep reading," Beatriz said as she sat on the bed and opened her legs. She flipped a bottle of lube open and applied a thin coating to her inner lips and inside her vagina. Ben stopped reading. He also stopped breathing.

"I can't read while you're doing that. Your vagina has rendered me illiterate."

Beatriz rolled her eyes, wiped her hands on a tissue and grabbed the book from him.

"It says," she said as she lay on the bed, her head propped up on two pillows, "that one of the more popular versions of modified missionary position is the butterfly. So we should try that one."

"A bee doing a butterfly? Is that even legal?"

"I'm sure it's legal. But it might be dangerous. At least for the butterfly." Beatriz turned a page in the book. "It says I lay on my back and you stand for this one. You can either hold me up by my ass or we can put pillows under my hips to raise them."

"Let's go for the pillows."

"You think I'm too heavy to lift?" she asked with a wicked gleam in her eyes.

"No, I just want my hands free to play with your boobs."

"Good point. This position is supposed to help the man 'give the clit the attention it deserves.' That's me quoting the book, by the way."

"I like this book. It's nice and friendly and tells me to touch your clit. I appreciate that."

"So does my clit. Ready?"

Ben glanced down. He was more than ready.

"Alright," Beatriz said. "Let's do it."

"Okay. We're going to do this." Ben stared

down at Beatriz on the bed. "What am I doing?"

Bea laughed, a big, luxurious laugh. "Why don't we start with foreplay? That might make you feel more comfortable."

"Yes, absolutely. Foreplay." Ben crawled onto the bed and lay on his side next to Beatriz. "Sorry, I've never had sex like this before."

"Like what?"

"Like with a professional who's taking notes, and we're preplanning everything. It's not spontaneous."

"Spontaneity in sex is overrated. I'm turned on already and all we've done is talk about the sex. Talking before can be the best foreplay. It's really sexy to plan sex."

"True. I like that I know what we're doing. Usually when you're with someone new, you have no idea what they like in bed. You start off in one position and you never know if that's her favorite or least favorite. Takes the pressure off a little to know ahead of time what the plan is."

"I'll let you pick the next position," Beatriz promised.

"I love this plan. I'm going to kiss you now. Are you ready?" Ben asked.

Beatriz closed her eyes and took a deep breath. She appeared to be meditating.

"I'm ready." She opened her eyes. "Let's do this."

"Okay. Here we go." Ben moved in closer to Beatriz and cupped the side of her face. For the past five minutes they'd been joking with each other. He did it to mask his nervousness. Impossible to think this beautiful, confident woman would be nervous. But now that the joking had stopped, his nervousness faded entirely. The only right thing to do at this very moment was to kiss her.

And he did.

Their lips met and at first Ben held back. They'd only kissed once before, the night they'd met and he'd shown her around campus. That had been a quick kiss, a mere promise of things to come. If he'd known it would be five years before he kissed her again, he never would have stopped that night.

She opened her mouth against his and he deepened the kiss. She tasted sweet and tart, like she'd been drinking orange juice. He pulled up and smiled down at her.

"Mimosa?" he asked.

"Blame Claudia," she sighed. "Do I need to go brush my teeth?"

He shook his head. "No. You taste amazing." Ben traced her bottom lip with his thumb. "Absolutely amazing."

Again they kissed, harder this time, heavier. Ben pulled Beatriz under him. He cupped the back of her head and kissed her neck and ears. His erection ground against her hip and she moved against him.

"Is everything okay to do?" he whispered. "Touching and kissing?"

"Anything you want," she said, equally breathless.

He kissed a path down the center of her chest and took her right nipple in his mouth. Beatriz weaved her fingers through his hair and arched her back.

"Nipple sucking..." Beatriz said, her voice low and heated, "is the greatest thing ever invented."

"You like it?" He paused long enough to smile up at her.

"Love it. Don't stop."

"Sorry." He kissed her right nipple again and teased it with his tongue. He held her left breast in his hand, squeezing it gently as his thumb stroked the nipple. Beatriz placed her arms over her head to give him full and unfettered access to the front of her body. He rose up on his hands and knees over her and took her left breast into his mouth as his right hand roamed down her stomach and settled between her thighs. She opened her legs and he easily found her swollen clitoris with his fingertips.

Beatriz flinched and smiled. "Did I do something right?"

"Very right. Keep doing it."

"Yes, ma'am."

He kneaded her clitoris with his fingers, watching as Beatriz moved her hips in conjunction with his touch. He loved the way she moved, like a dancer—strong and graceful and fearless.

"Can I go inside you?" Ben asked as he ran his fingertips along the wet seam of her vaginal lips.

"That's why we're here," she said with a seductive smile.

She spread her legs even wider, and Ben slid two fingers into her. Her slick passage offered no resistance as he pushed in as deep as he could.

"God, you feel as good as I dreamed you would." He probed inside her with his fingers, reveling in her incredible heat, her softness, the fluttering of her taut inner muscles.

"You dreamed of me?"

"All the time," he confessed. "I wanted you so much. It nearly killed me to back away from you. And then Claudia told me about your blog..." he said before he realized he'd just admitting to reading her sex toy reviews.

He pushed a third finger into her. Her body opened up further to receive it. He massaged her inside, in no hurry to do anything but get to know her vagina on the most intimate of terms.

"You read the Miss Bea Haven column?" She sounded pleasantly surprised, almost flattered.

"Of course not. A column where the sexiest woman on earth pleasures herself with sex toys and then writes about it? Gross."

Beatriz laughed and Ben grinned as her vaginal muscles twitched around his fingers.

"Did you pleasure yourself while reading about me pleasuring myself?"

"Masturbate? Me?" Ben asked, feigning innocence. "Never. That's disgusting."

"If you masturbated while reading about me masturbating, I might have to masturbate while imagining you masturbating about me masturbating."

"Or we could just skip the masturbating and fuck each other."

"Better idea," Beatriz agreed.

Almost reluctantly, Ben pulled his fingers out of Beatriz. He could have touched her inside all night. But they had a job to do. The best job in the history of the universe, specifically.

Ben started to pull away from her, but Beatriz stopped him with a hand on the one part of his body certain to stop him from moving a muscle.

"My turn," she said, stroking him. "You touched me. Now I get to touch you."

"That's entirely fair," Ben said as he rolled onto his back. Beatriz moved her hand slowly over his inches, caressing him over and over again from base to tip.

"Does this feel good?" she asked.

His abdominal muscles tightened like a coiled spring and he let out a groan from the back of his throat. "If you keep doing that, I'll come in your hand," Ben warned her.

"Oh. No. Anything but that."

"I thought we were doing the butterfly."

"We are," she said. "But I like getting to know your body."

"It is beyond pleased to make your acquaintance."

Beatriz finally released him. Good timing, too, as he was getting precariously close to orgasm. She slid on top of him and put her hands on either side of his head.

She dipped her head and kissed his lips while he brushed her long dark hair over her sculpted shoulders.

"Are you ready to be inside me?" she asked.

She asked the question with sincerity, and he answered with equal sincerity while looking into her eyes.

"Yes."

He kissed her and held her close for a moment. He couldn't believe it was finally happening. For years she'd been the one who got away and now here she was, in his arms, waiting for him to make love to her.

No. Stop. This was just sex, Ben reminded himself. Beatriz had even called it work. He shouldn't get all wrapped up emotionally in this. Sex. Fucking. Just that.

He almost convinced himself. Almost.

She moved off him and Ben slowly stood up. He rolled on a condom while Beatriz lined up her hips with the end of the bed and put two pillows under her pelvis.

"Stand right there," she said, pointing at the floor. "I need to put my ankles on your shoulders. Sorry if my feet smell weird."

Ben took her ankles in his hands.

"Horrible. Can't even breathe," he said before turning and kissing the top of her right foot.

"Okay, whenever you're ready, I'm ready," she said as she scooted an inch closer to the end of the bed. He looked down at her, at the absolute splendor of her nakedness, her breasts and hard nipples, her soft flat stomach and rounded hips, her hair against the sheets, black on white. He took his erection in his hand and guided it to the opening of her vagina.

Slowly he eased into her, wanting to relish every second of this moment, of this first penetration. He slid in until his hips were flush against her bottom and he felt the hard stop of her cervix barring him from going any deeper.

Closing his eyes, he took a few deep, heavy breaths to calm himself. He opened them and saw Beatriz looking up at him.

"You're smiling," he said.

"You're inside me."

"That's why I'm smiling, too. Does it feel okay?"

She nodded. "Deep. It feels really deep." She lifted her hips and he bumped against her cervix again.

"Too deep? I can pull out."

"Try thrusting. We'll see how it feels."

He pulled out and pushed back in again. He'd never seen anything sexier in his life than the sight of his cock moving in and out of Beatriz. Her wetness coated him, her heat consumed him. He ran his hands up and down her long legs. He found her clitoris again and teased it with a single fingertip. The combination of penetration and clitoral stimulation seemed to do magical things to Beatriz. Her fingers clutched the sheets and her hips moved up and down his penis. He barely had to move now. She did most of the work.

"Good?" he asked.

"So good. Can you hand me my phone?"

"What?"

"My phone. By the bed. Can you reach it?"

He could reach it, easily. He handed it to her and she tapped on the screen.

"Sorry," she said. "Part of the job."

"Are you texting somebody while we're having sex?"

"Notes," she said. "Just takes a second."

"This is for the review?"

"Posterity demands it." She tossed her phone aside and smiled up at him. "Seriously. Sorry about that. I should have warned you."

"What did you write?"

"Just notes."

"Bea..."

She took a quick breath. "I wrote that this position is highly recommended for lights-on sex as you get to see your partner's amazing body in all its glory."

"I noticed that. You look incredible."

"I was talking about you," she said.

Ben started to say something funny, something snarky, then stopped himself. Nothing came out except a grinning, slightly sheepish, "Thank you."

Beatriz said nothing to his "thank you," only continued to gaze at him, eyes glowing with heated desire.

"There's another note you should make," he said. "For the guy, this position is awesome because he can watch himself moving in and out of her. I mean, you. I mean, I can see all of you, and it's sexy as hell."

"Really?" she asked.

"Seriously. I can't stop looking."

Beatriz picked up her phone again and

handed it to him. "Take a pic," she said. "It'll last longer."

He stared at her. "Are you serious?"

"You think only men enjoy porn?" she asked. "The pic is for me. If you're lucky, I might email it to you."

"I'm inside you. I am officially the luckiest man on the planet."

He took her phone and snapped a few quick pictures of their bodies joined together. He gave her the phone back and she tossed it aside.

"Make me come, and I'll send it to you," she said.

"Challenge accepted."

He started to thrust with intensity again. He couldn't get enough of fucking her.

He rubbed her clitoris as he pushed into her, harder and faster. Beatriz closed her eyes. She seemed to lose herself in the pleasure of the moment, running her hands down her stomach, cupping her own breasts, lifting them, pinching her nipples and moaning in breathless little pants. He increased the speed and pressure of his ministrations to her clitoris, a move that caused Beatriz to gasp loudly. Her body went stiff for a moment before she released a loud, lusty cry. Her vagina spasmed with her climax around Ben's still-thrusting length.

Beatriz took a few calming breaths.

"Okay," she said, still panting. "Your turn."

Ben kissed her calf. "Is it cheating if I get on my knees? I'm not sure I can come in this position." He had to concentrate so hard on keeping her legs on his shoulders that he doubted he could focus enough to orgasm while both standing and holding her legs up.

"You can do whatever you want," she said. "The butterfly position has been tried, tested and woman-approved."

Laughing, Ben pushed Beatriz back on the bed so he could kneel on the mattress. He lowered her legs down to either side of him and held her hips.

"This position is called the Anvil according to the book." Beatriz grabbed the book lying on the bed and flipped it open.

"The Anvil?"

"Don't ask. It makes no sense to me either." She flashed him a picture of a couple having sex in the same position they were in—woman on her back, man on his knees, her ankles on his shoulders. She tossed the book aside and adjusted her legs. "Thanks for the orgasm. I guess I owe you a picture."

"You're even sexier when you're coming," Ben said as he put his whole body into his thrusts.

"I want to see you come."

"You will. I'm so close. I love fucking you."

"Good. I'll need you to do it again tomorrow."

"Call my secretary. We'll see if I can fit you into my schedule." He winked at her. Neither Heaven nor Hell nor pre-wedding festivities was going to keep him out of Beatriz's bed and body this week.

Ben took Beatriz's breasts in his hands and held them while he moved against her and inside her and with her. She'd already had her orgasm, but she still moved, raising her hips to meet his thrusts, coaxing him on and on. He lost himself inside her, lost all self-consciousness, all nervousness, all fear. Their bodies merged seamlessly. He belonged inside her. Long, slow strokes turned into sharp, hard, fast thrusts. He pounded into her shamelessly, mercilessly, her hungry sounds of pleasure driving out any fear that she wasn't enjoying this as much as he was. On his knees, leaning over her with his hands on her breasts, Ben came with a guttural grunt that did no justice to the incredible pleasure of the orgasm that shot through him from neck to knees.

He collapsed on top of Beatriz and rolled them onto their sides. For a long time they merely lay together in a tangle of arms and legs as they tried to catch their breath.

Ben felt a sense of peace, of perfect happiness coming over him. They had only this week together and he was determined to spend every free second inside her.

"So..." he said at last as Beatriz stretched out next to him, her thigh over his stomach, her head on his chest where it belonged.

"So?"

"That was chapter two?"

"Chapter two," she said.

"How many chapters are in this book?"

"Twenty."

"Wedding's in five days. Twenty chapters. Four chapters a day."

"We can skip some."

He shook his head. "Oh, no, if we're going to review this book, we're going to review it right."

Beatriz laughed and laid her head back on his chest.

"I love my job," she said.

CHAPTER SIX

"Holy…" Beatriz said as Ben pulled out of her and collapsed onto his back. He hit the mattress with his hand hard enough to rattle the headboard.

"That's it. I'm tapping out for the night. Sorry."

"Sorry? We just had sex three times in four different positions." Beatriz laughed and bit his shoulder. God, he had beautiful shoulders. And now he had beautiful bite-marked shoulders. Even better.

With languid limbs she pulled herself into a sitting position and grabbed her phone.

"I was hoping for five," he said. "Ben Junior isn't going to make it."

"That's okay. The Queen Bee is tapping out, too."

"You call your vagina the Queen Bee?"

"She's in charge most of the time. Okay, so what did we do? Butterfly."

"Butterfly," Ben repeated. "The Anvil."

"Anvil, got it." She tapped on her phone screen. "I have no idea where these names come from, by the way."

"We did the Figure Eight, right?"

"That's the only one where the name actually made sense." Beatriz made another note.

"What was that last one?" Ben asked. "It was weird."

"Coital Alignment. Some sex doctors invented it in the eighties, I think. It's supposed to maximize clitoral stimulation."

"Is that why you came twice during it, and I felt like I was going to fall out of the bed the entire time?"

"I wasn't complaining." Beatriz winked at him. Ben got out of bed and headed for the bathroom. As soon as he was gone she sunk back into the bed and stared up at the ceiling. It had happened. She and Ben had finally had sex. Five years she'd wondered what had gone wrong between them, why he'd backed off, what she'd done wrong. What was wrong with her that he wouldn't sleep with her when she offered? What red-blooded, straight college senior turned down sex with a naked eighteen-year-old woman standing right in front of him? One perfect date, one perfect kiss and then...nothing?

But at least now she knew the reason. She forgave Ben, of course, and Henry, too. It had been long enough that there was no reason to hold a grudge against either of them. But more than that, those years apart disappeared as soon as he started talking, as soon as he smiled. He was still the same Ben she adored from back then. He'd only grown more handsome in their time apart. He wore his dark blond hair in a shorter style, which made his blue eyes the focal point of his face. In college he always wore stubble on his chin to look older. Now he shaved to look sophisticated. He'd been a party boy in college, a little too much beer and not enough working out. Now he'd slimmed down by about ten pounds and had nothing but muscle on his six-foot frame. Adulthood, the real world—it definitely looked good on him.

And good Lord, the sex had been so good it almost made her angry. They could have been fucking like that years ago if he'd told Henry to shove it. Well, no need to stay pissed. They had all week to make up for lost time.

The sound of running water in the bathroom stirred her from her reverie. Sounded like Ben was about to hop in the shower. Maybe she should surprise him...

Beatriz started to get out of bed but stopped when her phone buzzed.

She grinned at the text message from Claudia.

So...? it read.

She tried to think up a suitable reply to Claudia's not-so-subtle message. Instead of typing anything back, she took a quick picture of the three ripped condom wrappers on the bedside table and sent it to her.

Claudia quickly wrote back.

Damn. TMI, she said, although Beatriz knew Claudia wanted all the details she could get.

I could have sent you the other pic we took, Beatriz texted back.

Claudia answered with a simple, *GROSS!*

Laughing, Beatriz tucked her phone away. She had Ben to attend to.

She crawled out of bed, already pleasantly sore inside and out. It had been a while since she'd had that much sex. Back in Spain she'd had a lover, a widower in his forties who'd wanted nothing but no-commitment sex to serve as a distraction from his grief. They'd been friends and lovers and nothing more. But she'd moved back to the States over two months ago and hadn't bothered pursuing anyone while she settled into her new apartment outside of Washington, D.C., and reconnected with friends. She'd forgotten how much she missed sex. Orgasms she had every day, and while she enjoyed them, those solo satisfactions could never completely replace the pleasures to be found lying naked underneath a man like Ben, her thighs open to receive him into her, her body a gift given to him, his body a country to be endlessly explored.

While she was stretching her back, Ben peeked his head around the wall by the bathroom. He crooked his finger at her.

"What?" she whispered.

"Come here," he whispered back.

"Why are we whispering?" she asked.

"I have no idea."

She followed his beckoning finger into the bathroom where Ben had drawn a bath in the large Jacuzzi tub. "Are you trying to get me wet?" she asked.

"Soaking wet," he said, and then with a heroic flourish swooped her up in his arms. Beatriz squealed with surprise as Ben feigned dropping her in the water. Instead, he set her gently in the tub and stepped in behind her.

With a blissful sigh, Beatriz lay back against his chest as Ben wrapped two strong, wet arms around her.

"Bath. Good idea," she said.

"Purely therapeutic," Ben said. "I think I overworked an ass muscle during a figure-eight grinding maneuver."

"I'll put that warning in the review notes."

"I can't believe you're going to write about us fucking for this blog."

"Why not?" she asked. "I won't put your name in it."

"Your name's in it."

"I know. But I don't care. It's not like it's some big secret that women masturbate and have sex."

"You'd think it was, the way people act about sex."

"Someone has to talk about sex like it's just any other normal human activity. If no one else wants to do it, I guess that means I have to," she said.

"How did you get to be like this?" Ben

asked as he scooped up handfuls of warm steaming water and poured them over her chest.

"Like what?"

"Like this sex goddess who writes about sex, studies sex, reviews sex toys... I mean, how did you decide to go into that field?"

Beatriz laughed and sighed as Ben massaged her breasts with his soapy hands. "Well, you know I was born in El Salvador," she said. "Lived there until I was ten."

"I know. You told me about all the fighting and civil unrest."

"After my parents died, my grandparents did everything they could, spent every penny they had to get me to the States. America is free, they said. You can do anything in America, be anything you want in America. In my country, a woman who was raped couldn't get an abortion, even if the pregnancy would kill her."

"That's crazy.'

"It's a beautiful country, so much to love. But it's hard to live there as a woman. Then I came to the United States, and I decided that I would use all the freedom my grandparents had worked so hard to give me. So my senior year in high school, it's almost time for prom.

And the school starts to freak out because the guidance counselor says they should have condoms at the prom. This counselor, Mr. Lear, was such a good guy. Not judgmental. He said teenagers would drink no matter what parents and teachers did, so they should offer a prom-night taxi service. And teenagers would have sex no matter what parents and teachers said, so the school should supply condoms."

"What happened?"

"He was fired."

Ben sighed. "No surprise there, I guess."

"But I was a student, so I knew they couldn't fire me. I bought fifty boxes of condoms and put them on the tables at prom. I got in so much trouble for that."

"You rebel." Ben laughed so hard he made a wake in the bathwater.

"My foster parents fought for me, stood up for me. I got suspended but not expelled. Apparently they couldn't find any school rules that said students couldn't give other students condoms."

"You're my hero right now," Ben said, running his hands over her thighs. She did love his hands.

"I'm no hero. I just couldn't believe that people in this country were so afraid of sex.

We have all this freedom in America—freedom people fought and died for—and we're so afraid to exercise it. We're afraid to talk about things that might offend other people, afraid to do what we want because someone might call us a 'slut.' Truth is, I get nothing but fan mail from women who thank me for talking about sex and helping them find ways of making their sex lives better. When I'm having good sex, I'm the happiest, least violent person on earth. If people had more and better sex and felt less guilty about it, we'd live in a much better world."

"I am happy to help you in your quest to fuck for world peace."

"I'll take you up on that offer," Beatriz said.

"I do think it's amazing that you came by yourself to the U.S. when you were that young."

"My grandparents knew Claudia's father through his work. When you're that young, it's an adventure. It took me until I was sixteen to realize I wasn't ever going back."

"I'm sorry all that happened to you," Ben said. "I wish you'd had an easier life. But I can't say I'm not happy you ended up here.

And by here, I mean naked in this bathtub with me."

"I'm glad I'm here, too. And by 'here' I mean in the States. And naked in this bathtub with you."

Ben cupped her breasts and kissed her neck. "And I'm sorry it took me so long to do this." He nipped softly at her shoulder and Beatriz laughed.

"*Más vale tarde que nunca,*" she said.

Better late than never.

Beatriz turned around in the bathtub to face Ben on her hands and knees. She kissed him long and hard as his wet hands dug deeply into her hair.

"I won't make you fuck me again," she said, smiling against his lips. "But I wanted to kiss this gorgeous face."

"Make me fuck you again? Anything but that," he said. "I have a better idea."

He grabbed her around the waist and sat her on the edge of the tub. She leaned back as he pushed open her legs.

"Wait," she said as he started to touch her.

"Wait?"

"We need the book."

"I know how to go down on a woman. I don't need a book to tell me."

"Yes, but we're doing this for the book review. We have to at least read the chapter on it before we do it so I can use it in the article."

Ben sighed and put his face in the water for a second. Beatriz grabbed him by the back of the hair and forced his face out of the water.

"You stay there," she said to him. "I'll get the book."

She was gone and back in seconds. With the book in her hand she sat back on the widest edge of the tub and put her leg on the side.

"Sorry," she said. "It's work. You understand."

She laughed as he groaned. God, she did love torturing this sexy man. She flipped through the book and found the page on oral sex.

"Good stuff in here," she said. "The first part is hygiene-related. We can skip that."

"We're doing this in a bathtub," Ben said as he rubbed her inner thighs. "I don't know how much more hygienic we can get."

"Then it says to use the fingers first. The labia are sensitive," she read. "For better or worse. Start slow by massaging the outer lips. As she grows more aroused, her labia will swell and bloom like flower petals."

"It does not say that."

"It does!" She flipped the book around and pointed at a sentence.

"So it does. Flower massage it is then." Ben cupped her between her legs and she pushed into his hand. He moved in closer and knelt between her wide-open thighs. With both hands he massaged her vulva from the back of her thighs to her clitoris. Before she knew it, she had started to pant again.

"Okay, that does feel really good."

"Are you blooming?" Ben asked.

"Spring has sprung."

Through half-closed eyes, Beatriz watched Ben's fingers stroking her skin.

"What else does the book say?" he said.

She lifted the book again. "It says, '*Spread the vaginal lips open with the fingertips. Lick the vagina from the base to the clitoris. Go slowly. Ask her to tell you what feels the best and focus most of your attention there.*'"

"Good advice," Ben said as he used his thumbs to spread her wet folds open wide. He dipped his head between her legs and licked her as the book instructed. Beatriz moaned as his tongue slid across her, up and down and up again. "You taste amazing," he said.

"You feel amazing."

He pushed his tongue in deeper. She felt it burrowing into her, and all she wanted to do was throw her legs wider and wider to welcome him.

"What feels good?" Ben asked as his lips pressed a burning kiss into her entire clitoral region.

"That," she gasped. "Right there."

He ran his tongue around her clitoris in slow circles before sucking it between his lips. Beatriz searched for something to hold on to, something to grip to steady herself. She found nothing but Ben so she held onto him. Wrapping her hands around his wrists, she clung to him as his mouth did miraculous things to her. She wanted to beg for more, wanted to beg him to put his cock inside her again, but she restrained herself. First of all, they were both slightly sore from all the sex. And second, she couldn't believe how good he was at going down on her. She might have to put a note in her review that no matter how good a sex book was, it could never beat having a partner who knew what he was doing.

And damn, Ben knew what he was doing.

Ben slipped a hand between her legs and slid one finger inside her. He tickled her from the inside out and she squirmed with pleasure.

He probed inside her until he found that one spot that always made her wince with ecstasy when touched.

"Don't stop," she begged. "Keep doing that."

"Until my tongue falls off," he said before kissing her again with renewed enthusiasm.

Everything inside Beatriz started to tighten. Tighter...tighter...the pleasure was so acute it almost hurt. She felt waves of pleasure converging, like water surging against a dam, pleasure and pressure building. She put her hands on the side of the tub and lifted herself a few inches up, her body wanting, needing, to rise as desire washed over her.

Finally the dam broke, and with a loud cry she came hard in Ben's mouth. The orgasm shook her whole body and dissipated slowly.

Ben sat up on his knees and licked his lips. Beatriz leaned in and kissed him, tasting herself on his mouth.

"I'll return the favor whenever you want," she said.

"Are you going to blow me while holding a book in your hand?" he teased.

"I don't need the book for that." She winked at him.

"So this isn't just about work, then?" he asked, the smile gone from his face.

The earnestness of the question and the look on his face caught her off guard. Now she had to answer. Was this about more than the book review? Or was this just a week of sex before parting ways again?

"Work," she said. "I just meant...you know, I already read that chapter," she lied.

"Oh," Ben said. "Got it." He lay back in the water and scrubbed his face and hair.

It was just work, right? Beatriz thought. This couldn't go anywhere. They lived on opposite coasts. Even thinking about this being more than work was pointless. She put it out of her mind. This was sex. This was work.

Nothing more.

CHAPTER SEVEN

Ben woke up in a strange bed. But it was the wrong strange bed. At least, it wasn't the strange bed he'd been hoping to wake up in this morning. Last night after their bath he'd dallied in Beatriz's room, talking until she started yawning, in the hopes she'd invite him to sleep with her. He was on West Coast time so her midnight was only his nine o'clock. Still, he would have willed himself to sleep at such an ungodly early hour for the privilege of waking up next to Beatriz. After one last kiss she'd shooed him out of her room, claiming she'd never stop groping him long enough to get any sleep if he didn't go, scoot, vamoose.

"This is supposed to convince me to leave?" he'd asked.

The pillow she threw at him convinced him to leave.

Now that morning had come and Ben lay alone in his hotel room bed, he could do nothing but stare up at the ceiling. Stare and wonder...

"This is a bad idea," he said aloud to the empty room. "Isn't it?" he asked, and waited for an answer. "She's in D.C. now. I'm in L.A. That's a good sign, right? That we both live in towns known by their initials?"

Ben exhaled heavily.

"I'm an idiot. And this is a terrible idea, Ben," he told himself. He felt that by speaking the words out loud, there might be a chance of him taking his own advice. "You didn't want this, remember? You didn't want to get serious with someone so soon. You have a great job and a great life. You're not a broke college kid anymore. Things are good. Why complicate your life with some kind of long-distance relationship?"

A good question. A great question. One Ben made the mistake of answering.

"Because Bea is beautiful, and she's smart, and she's sexy as hell and funny and amazing... And you're *not* a broke college kid anymore. You have a real job now. You can afford a long-distance relationship. Complicated? What the fuck is complicated about being with an amazing woman like Bea? Nothing. You just did it. Right?" Ben asked himself.

Right.

Ben started to get up. He paused, looked at the clock, and rolled back down again.

"She said it was just work," he reminded himself. "Did she mean that, or is she doing the 'I don't want to get hurt again by you, you asshole' thing? Which I deserve."

Ben did deserve it. He'd been so single-minded about getting a good job after college that he didn't even let himself consider having a serious relationship back then. Nothing was going to get in the way of his ticket to freedom. Not even Beatriz.

But things were different now. He had the career, had the freedom. Now maybe if he played his cards right, he could have Beatriz, too.

"When I said I was done with all women for at least a year," he addressed himself, "I meant all women but Beatriz. I just didn't specify that at the time."

At that moment his phone buzzed. He picked it up and smiled at the text message from Beatriz. *What are you wearing?*

Ben, as usual, had slept naked.

Leather chaps, he wrote back. *And a clown nose. Don't ask.*

What are you doing? Beatriz texted.

Soliloquizing, which autocorrect tried to change to "solo quizzing."

Is that what they're calling it now? We used to call it masturbating.

I masturbate with a Shakespearean accent, Ben replied. *I have no idea what that means.*

Me neither. Want a blow job in the shower?

Business or pleasure? Ben wrote back before adding a vital caveat. *Never mind. My cock just told me it doesn't care why. Coming.*

Yes. Yes you are, Beatriz responded.

Ben pulled on yesterday's pants and yesterday's shirt and didn't bother with yesterday's underwear, yesterday's shoes or yesterday's socks. He did brush his teeth, which was as much for his benefit as Beatriz's. In five minutes he was pounding on her door.

"That was fast," she said, holding the door open for him. She had nothing on but a towel.

"I didn't want to miss you blowing me in the shower. I'm not late, am I?" He started unbuttoning his shirt.

"I'm not even in the shower yet."

"Then hurry up," he said, throwing his shirt off. "You're late."

Ben stepped into the shower and Beatriz joined him. He wrapped Beatriz in his wet arms and kissed her hard and deep. She tasted like toothpaste and heat. He pushed her under the shower, soaking them both as he drank the water off her lips and neck.

"I didn't get to read the blow job chapter in the book," he said.

"Don't worry. I read it," she said, wrapping her hand around him and stroking. He breathed deep as he grew even harder in her hand.

"What did it tell you to do?" Ben asked, slightly panting as she stroked him from base to tip and back again.

"This," she said, and went down on her knees in front of him. She held him by the base while her lips focused their attention on the tip of his penis first, licking and teasing it while her hand gave it gentle squeezes. The blood started pounding and he grew thicker as she took him deeper into her mouth. Had he ever seen anything sexier in the world than her full lips surrounding him? No. No, he hadn't.

She took every inch of him into her

mouth, until he nudged the back of her throat. He started to pull back, not wanting to choke her, but she grabbed him by the hips and held him in place. She sucked him deep before letting go to lick him again and again. He reached down to touch her face but Beatriz grabbed his hand and placed it on the back of her neck. He took the hint and started to move his hips in small undulations, fucking her mouth with careful, controlled thrusts.

A breathy "yes" escaped his lips along with a few more grunts and gasps of pleasure. He never recalled being this vocal during sex before. Then again, he never recalled having this much fun during sex before.

Beatriz took his full length into her mouth again and cupped his testicles. Within a matter of seconds he teetered on the edge of coming. He held back, though, took a few deep breaths. He wanted to enjoy this moment as long as he could. As long as he could was about thirty seconds more. Beatriz's hands on him, her mouth all over him, the heat of her tongue, the wetness of her lips... It all felt so good he couldn't hold on anymore.

"Bea," he gasped as a warning. Gentlemen always warned.

Beatriz ignored the warning. He came

hard in her mouth and she swallowed every drop of him.

She turned her face up and let the water cascade over her skin. He pulled her back to her feet.

"That was..." he began. "No. I'm done. I don't have the words. You sucked my vocabulary out with my cum."

"You don't need to talk anyway. I've got better plans for your mouth." She kissed him again, kissed him as if she meant it—the best kind of kiss.

After they finally broke off the kiss, Beatriz turned around and handed him the shampoo. He had way too much fun washing her long, thick hair. The back scrub turned into a massage. As the water poured down on them, they kissed and touched and licked and held each other until Beatriz pulled back and kicked him out of the shower. He apparently took up too much room for her to shave her legs. Outside the bathroom, he dried off and dressed in yesterday's clothes again. As soon as Beatriz emerged wearing nothing but a towel in her hair, he kissed her goodbye.

"I have to go back to my room and change," he said.

"I'll see you at lunch."

"We can go in together," he offered. "You know, like a date."

"A date? Us? Together?"

"Is that weird?"

"Incredibly," she said, but he saw the twinkle of amusement in her eyes.

"So no?" Ben asked.

"We're not dating. We're not a couple. I don't want people to think something's going on that isn't," she said.

Ben stared at her. "I just came in your mouth."

"Okay, good point," she said, smiling. "Lunch it is then. Come back here when you're ready?"

"Absofuckinglutely." He kissed her again and left her naked and wet in her hotel room. Why was he always doing that? Walking away from her when she was naked? He considered this habit a personal failing, on par with heroin addiction or serial killing, something to be overcome as soon as thoroughly as possible. He'd get medical attention if necessary.

He changed clothes in his room. He gave himself a once- and then twice-over in the mirror. Lunch was a casual affair today. He'd put on khaki shorts and a fitted T-shirt, which was his usual day-off uniform. July in upstate New

York. He had every right to wear shorts, right? And he did have good calves, or so his ex-girlfriend always told him. But was this outfit too casual? Would Beatriz like it? Would she think he looked homely? Or would she think he looked cool and confident?

"Oh, my God," he said to himself. "I'm a man. Men don't worry about their outfits."

He changed clothes twice more before leaving the room. When he knocked on Beatriz's door he was wearing slacks and an Oxford shirt.

Beatriz answered the door wearing shorts and a T-shirt.

"Dammit," Ben said after one glance at her.

"Hello to you, too, stranger," she said, letting him in the room.

"Sorry. I had shorts on and then I thought it was too casual."

"It's just lunch. And it's July. And you have great calves."

"I told myself all of that."

"Start listening to yourself," she said and kissed him. "Here. How about this?" Beatriz pulled off her shirt and shorts, took off her bra, and changed quickly into a strappy sundress. "Feel better now?"

"I just saw your boobs."

"So...?"

"I feel much better now."

They walked into the hotel restaurant together. Ben wanted to walk in holding Beatriz's hand but she'd been hesitant to even go to lunch with him. He decided not to push it. He hadn't told anyone that he and Beatriz were having sex this week. No one knew, and apparently Beatriz wanted to keep it that way.

"Hi, kiddos," Henry said as they took their places at the table. "You all find something fun to do last night? Movie? Evening stroll?"

"No, we just fucked a lot," Beatriz said after putting in an order for tea.

Ben nearly choked on his water. Henry and Claudia laughed. Apparently they both were well aware of what the two of them had been up to.

"Sorry," Ben swallowed his water without further incident. "I tried to talk her into the movie, but she would have nothing of it. She used and abused me instead."

"Poor dear," Claudia said, patting his cheek. "You can stay with me and Henry. We won't let the big bad Bea hurt you anymore."

"Thank you, Claudia. I appreciate that.

Your sister's an animal," Ben said, and Beatriz put an ice cube down the back of his shirt.

Lunch was a festive affair, everyone talking and laughing at once. Ben gorged on food. He usually never ate this much, but he figured he'd lost about two pounds just in semen in the past twenty-four hours. Might as well dive in. The rest of lunch he spent talking with the other groomsmen, friends of Henry's from his work. He already knew Mark, Henry's brother. They all promised Mark they would not allow the wedding planner to oust him as best man just because he was shorter than the rest of them. Mark thanked them profusely. He said that it was only fair that Henry got the height gene as he took the brains gene. Henry agreed.

Even as they talked and joked, Ben kept glancing over at Beatriz. The sun had come out and cast a golden light through the windows. He couldn't stop staring at this beautiful woman and remembering how she'd looked naked underneath him, her skin flushed with desire, her nipples hard and her breasts pert, her flat stomach quivering from an orgasm as her clitoris pulsed against his fingers.

And then Ben had an erection.

Dammit.

He willed it away by concentrating on his drink, on his conversation, on the faces of the other groomsmen. He looked at Henry making an obscene gesture with a French fry. That helped. Erection gone. He kept his eyes off Beatriz. This was lunch, a wedding lunch. He needed to focus on his groomsman duties and not think about Beatriz or sex or anything of the sort.

He felt a hand on his shoulder. Turning around he saw Beatriz standing behind him. She handed him a note written on a paper napkin and left the restaurant.

He opened the note.

Come fuck me, it read. *Chapter four is waiting for us.*

Far be it from him to disobey the direct order of a napkin.

"Gotta go, guys," he said. "Duty calls."

CHAPTER EIGHT

Henry rolled his eyes as Ben followed Beatriz out the door. Well, they'd lasted longer than he and Claudia would have under the same circumstances. Their first week together in college, he and Claudia both missed all their classes. They did nothing but have sex, sleep, eat, have more sex, more sleep, more sex, more eating. By the end of day seven, they were both dehydrated and severely chafed. Henry had even gone by the school clinic. The nurse on duty took one look at his red and chafed penis and told him no sex for a week. It was the longest week of his life.

Leaning over, he tapped Claudia on her leg.

"What's up?" she asked.

Henry leaned in and whispered. "Ben's dick and Beatriz's skirt. They just left."

Claudia glanced around the table to confirm their departure.

"Well, they lasted longer than we would have," she said. "More power to them."

"Am I out of the doghouse now?" he asked, running his hand over her bare thigh.

"We'll see…" she said. "Right now they're just having a bunch of sex. If they decide to stay together after the week is over, then you'll be completely out of the doghouse."

"We can have doggie style while I'm in the doghouse, right?" Henry asked.

"Of course."

"I might just stay in it then."

He kissed his fiancée and went back to eating French fries in the most inappropriate ways he could think of. He looked around the table and smiled with deep satisfaction. He'd initially balked at the idea of a big wedding. They could afford it, yes, but surely they could put their money to better use than hosting an event that was hardly more than a glorified party. But now he saw two high school friends talking to a college friend talking to a work friend. His brother, Mark, had his arm around his girlfriend's shoulders as they chatted with his grandmother and aunt, whom he hadn't seen in months. Even his mother and father looked relaxed for the first time in years. All they ever did was work, work, work. Their oldest son's wedding had forced them to take a week's vacation. Free time suited them. All these people were together, enjoying each other's company, all because he and Claudia had decided to have a big wedding. Everyone had brought gifts to celebrate their marriage. But this wedding was his and Claudia's gift to them—a reason to take time off work and just have fun with friends and family. He should get married every week.

He kissed Claudia on the cheek.

"I'll be right back," Henry said to her. His waiter had watered him like a damn plant at lunch.

"On your way back from the bathroom, could you stop by the front desk? I'm having something delivered."

"I'll check. Anything special?"

"Just stuff for the honeymoon," she said, and turned back to her conversation with his two favorite cousins.

After his trek to the bathroom, Henry stopped by the front desk. A bellhop asked him if he could offer his assistance.

"My fiancée said she was having something delivered to the hotel. Claudia Spears. Can you check?"

"Haven't seen anything come in today. You know what it is?" the bellhop, whose name tag read *KEATON*, asked.

"No. She just said it was stuff for the honeymoon. Clothes probably, or that fancy sunblock she always orders. I think it's just one box."

The bellhop disappeared into a back room. Five minutes later he returned with a box.

"Here you go," Keaton said. "Need a box cutter? Knife? Machete?"

Henry patted his pockets. He'd left his keys in the hotel room. "Yeah, thanks."

Keaton pulled out a small knife and sliced the tape on the box. Out of curiosity, Henry opened it and looked inside.

"What the hell?" he asked, staring at the contents of the box. Keaton peeked over his shoulder.

"Where are you going on your honeymoon? Sodom and Gomorrah?" the bellhop asked.

Inside the box Henry found three books:

- *The Good Girl's Guide to Pegging Your Man*
- *When He's Just Not Enough—A How-to Manual for Successful Open Relationships*
- *Swinging for Dummies*

And at the bottom of the box...a harness and dildo.

"That's a strap-on," Keaton said, reading the shock on his face. "Your girl must want to fuck you up the butt on your honeymoon."

"No way."

"You just got to use lube. Trust me on this."

Henry threw the books in the box and closed the flaps. He started to stalk toward the restaurant but stopped. Open relationships? Swinging? Claudia was going to wait until their honeymoon to tell him she wanted to sleep with other guys and fuck him up the butt? His stomach churned with anger and his head throbbed with fear. He wasn't enough for her? Their sex life wasn't enough for her?

He turned back around and headed for the elevators. Once in his room he paced back and forth for ten minutes trying to decide what to do. There was only one thing to do, he finally decided. The strong, manly thing to do.

Run for his life. And his butthole.

He picked up his phone and sent Claudia a text message.

The wedding is off.

CHAPTER NINE

Beatriz had only gotten her panties off by the time Ben knocked on her door. In her breezy un-underweared state she let him in, not giving him a chance to say a single word before she kissed him.

His hands were all over her. He stroked her back and her hair, grabbed her bottom and squeezed, caressed her nipples through the light fabric of her sundress.

"What's chapter four?" Ben asked as he pushed them toward the bed.

"It's various 'from behind' positions. Doggie style, et cetera."

"Chapter four is my new favorite chapter."

Beatriz grabbed the book off the nightstand and flipped through the pages as Ben kissed the back of her shoulders.

"What's it say?" he asked.

"Blah blah intensity," she read. "Blah blah penetration blah sitting blah standing blah lying down blah blah good view of the ass…"

"This chapter sounds pretty blah. Except for the ass part."

"Basically it just tells us the five different ways to do rear entry."

"I'm entering your rear?" Ben asked, not at all troubled by that prospect.

"Anal's chapter eight. We'll get to it tomorrow," Beatriz said. "Any preference?"

She showed him the page with all the illustrations. Classic doggie style with the woman on her hands and knees and the man kneeling behind her…standing rear entry with the woman bent over a table or the bed…lying down rear entry with the man stretched out on top of the woman, his chest to her back.

"I like that one," Ben said, pointing to seated rear entry, where the man sat in a chair and the woman sat in his lap.

"Worth a shot. Find a chair."

Ben pulled the comfiest looking hotel chair next to the bed. He started to undress, but Beatriz stopped his hands.

"I like sex with my clothes on sometimes. Makes it feel dirtier, you know," she said, her stomach fluttering with excitement. Making him come in the shower this morning had only whetted her appetite for more of him. "Is that okay?"

"As long as my dick's out and your panties are on the other side of the room, it's fine by me."

Beatriz picked up her underwear from where it was lying on the bed and tossed it at the door.

"Good enough?" she asked.

"I'd prefer them in the trash can, but it 'll do." He pulled her down onto his lap. Their mouths met and as they kissed, he pulled the strap of her sundress down, baring her breast. He tortured her lips with soft, playful bites. He kissed a path down her shoulder, cupped her breast, and brought her nipple to his mouth. She moaned as he licked her nipple. She loved watching him kiss her breasts. He always closed his eyes as if to concentrate on this most important of tasks. His long eyelashes rested on his cheeks. His tongue circled her areola. The man knew his way around a woman's body. She should write a thank-you note to every woman he'd ever fucked before. They'd taught him well.

He pulled down the other strap of her dress and gave her left breast equal attention until both her breasts felt heavy in his hands. Ben slid his hand under her dress and she opened her legs for him as best she could while sitting on his lap. He pushed two fingers in her and she moaned, already so wet for him she'd probably left a stain on his pants.

Ben massaged her G-spot, spiraling into her deeper and deeper until she felt him pressing against her pubic bone. It was the most delicious sensation. She should make a note of this to put in her book review. But her phone was all the way on the other side of the room. Fuck it. The review could wait.

As he teased her and played with her body, Beatriz held on to his shoulders, rubbed his strong arms and back through the fabric. She loved his body, couldn't get enough of it, couldn't get enough of him.

And that was bad. She only had him for a week, and once the week was over… Her heart stuttered when she thought that it would happen again, that Ben would walk away from her and she'd have to watch him go. Maybe using him as her book review partner had been a bad idea. She was enjoying this way too much.

"Ready?" Ben asked and Beatriz hesitated only a moment before nodding her head, too turned on to even utter a coherent sentence. Even with all her second thoughts about what they were doing, she knew she wanted him inside her, needed him inside her. She rose up off his lap and Ben unzipped his pants. She stroked him a few times before sliding the condom down over him. He gripped her by the hips and turned her back to him. Carefully she lowered herself, waiting until she felt the tip of his penis against her soaking, swollen inner lips. Once she did she sank down onto him, sighing with the deepest pleasure as he impaled her.

"This is my favorite part," she sighed as she leaned back against his chest and he wrapped his arms around her.

"What is?" he asked, kissing her bare shoulders.

"The part where you're inside me."

Ben laughed, a warm, throaty laugh that made her toes curl. "Mine, too."

She moved slowly against him, wanting to stay like this all day long. She wished the wedding could be postponed, if just for a day or two, anything to give her and Ben more time together.

Ben brushed her hair off her back and over her shoulders. He kissed her neck, the center of her spine, bit her little bee tattoo. He took her hips in his hands and ground her against his lap as his cock tunneled deeper into her. He pushed her thighs wider apart, draping each leg over his knees. Beatriz groaned as Ben found her clitoris and pinched it between his thumb and forefinger. It swelled against his touch. The deep muscles in her vagina clenched around him as her clitoris throbbed against his fingers.

She reached down between her legs and touched him where he entered her. She felt so connected to him right now, and in more ways than just physically. So many men were intimidated by her sexual confidence and her work as a sex blogger. Her vibrators and dildos and array of sex books and erotica made them nervous, made them feel emasculated as one former lover told her. You shouldn't need all this stuff, he'd said, pointing at her sex toys. I should be enough for you.

Beatriz had smiled when she answered, But you're not.

So much for that guy. She didn't even remember his name.

Ben seemed to find her work funny and sexy, and he'd even admitted he masturbated reading her columns. Not what she'd ever intended, but she certainly couldn't complain about the mental image of Ben touching himself while reading about her touching herself.

"What would you do if I showed you my vibrator collection?" Beatriz asked as Ben rubbed tight circles around her clitoris.

"I don't know. Probably ask if I could use them all on you."

"Good answer." Beatriz relaxed against his chest again while Ben continued to play with her clitoris. She closed her eyes and focused on her own pleasure as scenes from last night's lovemaking flashed across her mind's eye. The memories morphed into fantasies. She'd love to take Ben to the very edge of sex where all the walls of shame and fear came down, where flesh met fantasy, where the two of them could tell each other all their secret desires and then live them out every night in their bed.

Every night of her life...

Beatriz orgasmed in near silence, the force of the climax sucking the air out of her lungs.

"Stand up," Ben whispered. "Put your hands on the bed."

Beatriz did as instructed. She'd do anything Ben told her to do. That was one of the fantasies she longed to share with him. Some nights she'd love it if he took total possession of her body, made her his toy, his pet, his plaything, his slave.

Ben pushed her sundress up and entered her again from behind. He thrust hard into her, hard enough she gasped a little. But she didn't ask him to stop or slow down or go easy on her. That was the last thing she wanted. She wanted to feel his cock ramming into her, wanted to feel like his desire for her had overridden his reason, restraint and self-control. She relished the feel of his fingers digging into her hips. She wanted to feel every inch of him as he pulled out and slammed back into her.

"Fuck," Ben breathed, his voice barely more than a strangled whisper. It was the sexiest word he could have uttered. She heard the echo of his pleasure in that one word, the primal cry of a man lost in ecstasy, lost in her. She steadied herself against the bed as best she could even as Ben pounded into her, putting his entire body into his brutal thrusts. She loved that about him. He was always so nonchalant, so relaxed and cool out in the world. But during sex he dropped all pretense and threw his whole being into pleasing her, and himself.

Pounding...pounding...she was lost in the pounding.... With a fierce final thrust Ben came, his hand on her shoulder, holding on to her as if she alone kept him from collapsing. Ben slowly pulled out of her as she remained bent over the bed, trying to catch her breath. The sex had ended, but the pounding continued.

"What the hell?" she asked.

"Shit," Ben said, laughing. "Someone's pounding on the door. Can you get that?"

"Bea, it's Claudia!" came a voice through the door.

"Just a second," Beatriz yelled back.

Ben disappeared into the bathroom while Beatriz pulled her dress up over her breasts and grabbed a tissue. She wiped herself off between her legs, pulled on the first pair of underwear she found and threw open the door.

Claudia rushed into the room and started pacing.

"What's wrong?" Beatriz asked, seeing the panic on Claudia's face. Ben came out of the bathroom looking much more put together than he had when entered it.

"Henry called off the wedding," Claudia

said, her face a mask of pure fear and shock.

"What?" Beatriz nearly shouted the word.

"What the fuck?" Ben asked, sounding as shocked as her.

"Henry got up at lunch to run to the bathroom. I asked him to stop by the front desk..." Claudia wrung her hands. "I got this text message from him."

She handed Beatriz her phone.

Beatriz stared at the message in disbelief.

"What's it say?" Ben asked.

"He says, 'The wedding's off. I'm sorry I'm not enough for you. Hope you find another man to swing with. If I wasn't enough for you, you could have told me before we started planning the wedding. I'm staying at another hotel. Maybe we can talk tomorrow. For now, don't even call me.'"

"What does he mean?" Ben demanded. "He's not enough for you?"

Claudia ran her hands through her hair and collapsed onto the bed.

"I don't know. I have no idea where any of this is coming from. I've never cheated on him, never wanted to. We've been together almost seven years. I didn't invite any old boyfriends to the wedding. I don't know what he's talking about. None of this makes sense."

"Did you try to call him?" Beatriz asked, putting her arm around Claudia.

"Yes, but he didn't answer. I tried ten times. The wedding's in four days. Our families are here. Our friends. Everyone. And he's just...gone. And he won't even tell me why."

Beatriz nearly burst into tears of pure sympathy. And she would have if she wasn't so furious at Henry.

"It's a good thing he's gone or I would rip his heart out and eat it for dinner," Beatriz said.

"Can we get his side of the story first?" Ben asked.

"There is no his side of the story," Beatriz said, enraged that Ben would even suggest there was a "his" side of the story. "Claudia's not cheating on him with anybody. What possible excuse could he have for acting like this?"

"Something set him off. Henry is the most boring man alive. He doesn't have a good enough imagination to be paranoid," Ben said. "I'm not saying he's right. Just—"

"Just what?" Beatriz demanded. "Just you and Henry pulling this college-boy bros-before-hoes bullshit again?"

"What are you talking about?" Ben asked.

"Back in college, you and Henry just went

off and decided you and I shouldn't be together. And now Henry's decided to dump Claudia and you're taking his side."

"I'm not taking his side, Bea. I'm just saying he has one."

"So you're saying he's right? That Claudia's cheating on him?"

"I'm not saying that." Ben raised both his hands in surrender. "I'm saying something must have set him off."

"He's decided to lose his fucking mind four days before the wedding. That's what set him off, Ben. You want to take his side?" Beatriz pointed at the door. "It's out there. Go find it. And when you find him, you two just have a nice life together. We're done with you both."

Ben stared at Beatriz. She could see the shock and hurt on his face.

"Look, you're right to be pissed at me," Ben said.

"Yes, I am. And that should be the end of your sentence," Beatriz said. Ben opened his mouth and closed it again. He turned his back on her and walked out. Nothing surprising there. He'd done it before. She should have known he'd do it again. "*Hasta la madre... I swear if Henry doesn't get his ass back here...*"

"I can't tell everyone this is happening. I can't," Claudia said, and Beatriz turned her attention back to her sister. "Everyone will freak out. Mom will have a heart attack."

"Oh, God, she will," Beatriz said. Their mother had burst into sobs last night just at the sight of Claudia and Beatriz standing side by side for the first time in over a year. Her girls, she cried. Her two beautiful girls… Mom cried at the drop of a hat. This constituted far worse than a simple hat drop.

"We'll tell everyone you've got mild food poisoning and you're not going to be able to leave your hotel room for a day or so," Beatriz said. "No one will know anything's up. They'll just think you and Henry are holed up while you're puking your guts out. Okay?"

"Okay," Claudia said and blew her nose extravagantly. "You and Ben were fucking when I knocked on the door, weren't you?"

"Like demon bunnies," Beatriz admitted. She gave Claudia a kiss on the forehead as she stood up.

"I'm sorry."

"Don't be. We were niney-nine percent finished by that point." She handed Claudia a bottle of water and a tissue. "And we're one-hundred percent finished now."

CHAPTER TEN

In the hallway outside Beatriz's room, Ben stood with his back resting on the wall and his hands balled up into fists. He would beat Henry to death for pulling this bullshit. Things were going so well with Beatriz, and Henry had to go and fuck it all up by flipping out on everyone. Claudia was in there sobbing her heart out while he was standing in the hallway eating his heart out. And Beatriz was pissed. Pissed enough to bust out the Spanish, and that meant business.

That sealed it. Henry was a dead man.

Ben checked the internet for all the hotels within a twenty-five-mile radius. He'd find Henry, haul him back by the scruff of his neck and throw him at Beatriz and Claudia's feet.

Let her accuse him of the "bros before hoes" mentality then.

Luckily Henry and Claudia had chosen this area of upstate New York for its small town beauty and unspoiled river vistas. That meant he had only ten hotels to comb through in the area on his hunt for Henry. Five were within walking distance. The other five would require getting an Uber or renting a car. He started with the furthest one out that he could reach by foot. No luck at the Umstead. No one claimed to have seen a deranged but roguishly handsome twenty-six-year-old man walking around accusing innocent women of mysterious crimes. Ben flashed everyone at the desk a picture of Henry and Claudia he had on his phone. No dice. The Capital Inn was also a big fail. He also struck out at the Pinehurst and the Washington. He bribed every clerk at every hotel to call him if Henry showed up.

Disappointed and disgusted, Ben returned to the Hotel Essex. The Essex desk clerk helped him round up a rental car, and Ben headed out again to the next town over and the other five hotels he wanted to check out. If he failed there, he didn't know what he would do. Check the airport maybe? Call the police? Hire a hitman?

Hitman—that sounded about right. "Henry, you asshole," Ben growled as he turned out of the hotel parking lot. Ben knew he should be seven inches inside Beatriz right at this moment, not out hunting down a runaway groom who'd decided to break up with his fiancée and reality on the same day.

He shoved all thoughts of Beatriz aside. He was a man on a mission—a mission to kill another man. He drove into the next town over and found the first hotel. Then the second. Then the third. After the fourth he stopped and called Henry again. No answer. Ben didn't find Henry at the fifth and final hotel, either. He hated the thought of returning to the Hotel Essex a failure. He would find and throttle Henry and he would do it for Beatriz. And Claudia. And him. And for Henry, too. And maybe he'd throttle him more just for the fun of it.

So Henry wasn't at any of the other hotels in town. Where else could the man be staying? Did he get a fake mustache, shave his head, and book himself under a fake identity? No way. Henry had a good heart and great work ethic, but Claudia was the brains of the operation. Ben had checked every hotel within any reasonable driving distance. Nothing to do but go back empty-handed and hope Henry came to his senses.

"Henry, if you cost me Beatriz again so help me..." Ben muttered as he returned the car to the rental office and walked the two blocks back to the Essex. "You're not smart enough to hide anywhere. Where the hell could you be?"

Once the words came out, Ben knew exactly where Henry was hiding.

He raced to the front desk of the Essex and rang the bell.

"Can you call up to Henry Bard's room?" he asked the clerk.

The clerk typed something into the computer.

"Which room? He's got two booked."

"I knew it." Ben slapped his hand on the counter. That bastard had booked a second room at the Essex under his own name. It was such a stupid hiding place it was actually smart. "I don't know. What are the room numbers?"

"I can't give those out, sir."

"Fine. Call both of them."

The clerk rang both hotel rooms. No answer.

"That's it, I'm killing him." Ben thanked the clerk for trying and started to wander around the lobby. The Hotel Essex had only six floors. Maybe he could walk the halls and knock on every single door until Henry answered. But then he ran the risk of knocking on the door of Henry's mom, Claudia and Beatriz's mom, the maid of honor, wedding guests. Knocking on doors wouldn't work. He just needed a room number. He'd give anything for a damn room number.

"Can I help you, sir?" came a voice from behind him. Ben spun around and saw a young man in a bellhop's uniform. His name tag read *KEATON*.

"Can you be bribed?" Ben asked, deciding to cut through pretense.

"Yes. Yes, I can," Keaton the bellhop said, giving Ben a jaunty salute.

"Good. Will a Jackson buy me a room number?"

"Tito?"

"Andrew."

"Janet?"

"Andrew."

"Fine," Keaton said. "But a Franklin

would buy you five room numbers. And my R-E-S-P-E-C-T."

"Do you actually work here or are you an escaped mental patient?" Ben asked.

"You really want to know?"

Ben shook his head. "Nope." He handed over the twenty-dollar bill to Keaton. "I'm looking for the new room number for Henry Bard. He's got two rooms booked."

"Got it," Keaton said. "You stay here. I'll do recon. If I'm not back in ten minutes, assume I've been captured. Save yourself."

Keaton started across the hotel lobby. He seemed to be walking as if the theme music to Mission Impossible played in the background. Ben rolled his eyes. Maybe if he tackled the guy he could get his twenty back.

The clerk didn't pay any attention to Keaton's antics. The bellhop got behind the desk and said something to the clerk. One minute later he was Mission Impossible-ing his way back to Ben.

"Room 515," Keaton said. "Booked it today."

"You sure?"

"I'm sure. He booked right after I gave him the box."

"Box? What box?"

"His lady had some box delivered to her. A box of books and crazy stuff."

"Crazy stuff?" Ben's heart raced. Maybe he'd finally discovered something useful.

"Crazy. Stuff. Lady stuff. Crazy lady stuff. Crazy lady you stick up the butt stuff, if you know what I mean."

"I have no idea what you mean and I don't want to know what you mean," Ben said. "But the box was addressed to Claudia Spears?"

"It was. Saw it with my own eyes."

"Thanks. Seriously." Ben slapped him on the arm and ran to the elevators. He had no idea what "crazy lady you stick up the butt stuff" was, but a mysterious box was at least some sort of motive for Henry's weird behavior.

Ben arrived at room 515 and banged on the door.

No answer.

He banged harder.

No answer.

He kicked the door.

Still no answer except for the woman in the room next door sticking her head out into the hall and glaring at him.

"Sorry," Ben whispered. "The guy in this room ran away from his wedding."

"Oh," the lady said. "Then break that damn door down if you have to."

"Thank you, ma'am."

He kicked and banged and finally the door flew open and Ben found Henry standing before him looking more heartbroken, downtrodden and miserable than he'd ever seen him.

"Henry, what the hell—"

"She wants to fuck me up the butt, Ben." Henry stepped forward and wrapped Ben in a hug. "Hold me."

"I'm going to kill you," Ben said, grabbing Henry by the shoulders and force-marching him into the room. "What are you thinking? Are you thinking? At all? Is anything going on in there?" he asked, knocking on Henry's head.

"I've been doing nothing but thinking," Henry said as he grabbed a box off the table. "Look. Claudia said she ordered stuff for our honeymoon. It came. This is what was in the box."

Henry turned the box over and let everything fall out onto the bed. Ben picked up the first book. It was a guide to couples in the swingers/wife-swapping lifestyle. Another book said it would help women find compatible sexual partners outside their marriage especially if the husband was bad in bed or impotent. Ben raised his eyebrow at Henry.

"I can get it up, I swear," Henry said. "Like five times a day. And she knows that."

The third book was a guide for women on how to use a strap-on dildo to have anal intercourse with the men in their lives. If that wasn't enough, the book came with its own harness and dildo, plus a small package of lubricant.

"She's never once said anything about our sex life not being enough for her," Henry said, collapsing into a chair. "She's never once said she wants to see other people. I asked her once if she wanted to try kinky stuff because she was reading that one kinky book."

"There's more than one."

"Whatever. She said no, that she just liked reading about it and didn't want to do it. Apparently she lied because my fiancée wants to have sex with other guys and fuck me up the butt."

"Maybe she just wants to fuck the other guys up the butt, and not you."

"If she's going to fuck any guy up the butt, it'll be me." Henry pointed at himself.

"I'd let her if I were you, man. She's

pissed. Crying her fucking heart out right now. And Beatriz is going to kill you and me both."

Henry winced. "I pissed Beatriz off? She's scary."

"She's Spanish-speaking pissed."

"I'm going to die, aren't I?" Henry asked.

"You are. She's furious at both of us. She thinks we're in this together, just like in college when you made me dump her."

"I didn't make you dump her. I asked you not to pursue her. You didn't even put up a fight."

"Yeah, well, I didn't have your parents' money. I didn't want to fuck up my one chance to get a decent job."

"Fuck that. You already had the job offer. You were just scared of dating someone who had it more together than you did. That's why you dated dumb girls and then broke up with them when you couldn't stand to be around them anymore. Beatriz would have made you work and think. I had a girlfriend in college. I still got a good job and had a great life. So don't blame me for you being a pussy over Beatriz. You like to think you were being all loyal to your best friend by staying away from her. We both know you were just scared of the real deal."

Ben couldn't speak. He only looked at Henry curled up in the chair looking more scared and miserable than he'd ever seen the man look in his life.

"When did you get so perceptive?" Ben asked.

"I'm not perceptive." Henry rolled his eyes. "I just saw through your bullshit."

"Which is the actual literal definition of perceptive."

"Fine," Henry said. "I'm perceptive. I'm also fucked. Up the butt, apparently." He swept his arm toward the bed and the pile of books and sex toys.

Ben stared at the books and sex toys on the bed. He had to admit it didn't look good for Claudia. He didn't have a problem with couples wanting to swing, choosing to be in open relationships or using sex toys. But Henry and Claudia were a nice, staid, stable, happy, monogamous, vanilla couple. Finding out his almost-wife wanted to sleep with other guys and use a strap-on on him and be in an open relationship would freak out anyone on the planet. Anyone except Beatriz probably. She probably already owned all these books. And he already knew she had sex toys and dildos and the like. In fact... the contents of the box looked like something Beatriz would have delivered to her, not Claudia.

"Dude, hand me the box," Ben said, and with a desultory sigh, Henry picked up the box and tossed it at him.

Ben examined the box for labels, for any clues at all. Henry and Keaton hadn't been wrong. The box was clearly addressed to Claudia Spears. But right after her name was the word "Attention." Attention who? Attention what? The rest of the sentence had been cut off.

"It says *'Claudia Spears,'*" Ben said, "but after it, the label says *'Attention'* like it was supposed to go to the attention of someone else."

Henry's eyes widened. "It does?"

"I wonder..." Ben looked at the UPS label again. The box had been sent by someone named John Prinz. He grabbed the hotel phone and called Beatriz's room number.

She answered on the first ring. "Ben?"

"Do you know some guy named John Prinz?"

"Ben, what the hell—"

"You can yell at me all you want later,"

Ben said. "Just answer the question. John Prinz? You know him?"

"Yeah, of course," she said. "He's the editor at The Daily Cocktail."

"Would he possibly have sent some stuff to the hotel care of Claudia Spears?"

"He said he had a box for me he was sending. Why?"

"He sent it."

"Fine. I'll get it later. What's going on—"

"Never mind," Ben said and hung up the phone on her.

He grabbed the books and the sex toys off the bed and shoved them in the box.

"You," Ben said, grabbing Henry by the collar of his polo shirt. "Come with me."

"Wait. What are you doing to me?"

"Saving your marriage. And getting Beatriz back. One of those is a higher priority than the other. I'll let you guess which."

CHAPTER ELEVEN

Beatriz stared at the phone in her hand. Ben had hung up on her without answering her questions. Fine. Whatever. Let him be that way. She had more important things to worry about, like how to best murder Henry and where to bury his body.

Claudia gasped as the two of them—Ben and Henry—entered the room. Beatriz could tell she wanted to run to Henry, but she held back. Her eyes had turned red from crying.

"Is this yours?" Ben asked Beatriz as he handed her the box. Beatriz looked into the box.

"*Guide to swinging, open relationships, pegging...*" she said, smiling for the first time in hours. "Dildo and harness. Yeah, this is the stuff John sent me, to see if I wanted to review them for the blog. Where did you get them?"

"Look at the label," Ben said as Claudia and Henry continued to eye each other warily.

"That stupid fucker," Beatriz said, half-laughing, half-groaning. "I told him to send it to me care of Claudia Spears since she'd booked the hotel room in her name. He sent it to Claudia. John, you *cabrón*."

"Those are your books and stuff?" Henry asked Beatriz.

"Yes, they're mine. Not Claudia's." She emptied the box out onto the bed.

"You thought those were mine?" Claudia demanded, looking at books and the sex toys. "You thought I wanted to be in an open rela-tionship?"

"You said you had stuff coming for our honeymoon," Henry protested. "I asked. This is the box they gave me."

"I ordered a new swimsuit and beach towels since I forgot to pack ours, Henry." Claudia nearly yelled the words.

"So you don't want to be a swinger?" Henry asked.

"No, I don't want to be a swinger."

"And I'm enough for you?"

"You are more than enough for me," Claudia said.

"So you don't want to fuck me up the butt?" he asked.

Claudia slapped a hand on her forehead.

"No, Henry. I do not want to fuck you up the butt. I mean, unless you wanted me to, and then we can talk about it, but I'd really rather not unless it can't be avoided."

"It's more fun than you think it would be," Beatriz said. She'd tried it before with an old boyfriend and they'd both thoroughly enjoyed the experience.

"Just use lots of lube," Ben said. Beatriz looked up at him with an arched eyebrow. He put on his most innocent face. "What?" he asked her. "It was a phase."

Beatriz said nothing. She turned her attention back to Claudia and Henry.

"Baby, I'm so sorry," Henry said. "The box had your name on it and I just... I'm an idiot."

"You had me scared to death. I've been crying for three hours," Claudia said. "What do you have to say to that?"

"I thought you were going to fuck me up the butt."

"Oh, come here, you ridiculous man." She wrapped her arms around him. "I was still your fiancée even after you dumped me, you know. I refused to believe you didn't love me anymore."

"And I still loved you even when I thought you wanted—"

"To fuck you up the butt. I know."

"Aww..." Ben said. "I love a heartfelt reunion."

"They should probably go have make-up sex," Beatriz hinted loudly. She and Ben needed to talk and needed to talk right now.

"We probably should," Henry said.

"Definitely," Claudia said. "Thank you, Ben. Thanks for finding him."

"Anytime. But if he does it again, he might be getting fucked up the butt whether he likes it or not." Ben glared at Henry. Henry blanched.

"We're going. Thank you both." Claudia grabbed Henry by the front of his shirt and dragged him from the room.

"So..." Beatriz said once they were alone again in her room, "just use lube?"

"I was bi for like a week in college," he said.

Beatriz sat on the bed and looked up at him.

"Thank you for getting Henry and

straightening this mess out," she said, feeling uncharacteristically nervous around Ben. They'd been having sex only five hours ago, but that was before Henry decided to turn the world upside-down.

Ben shrugged and shoved his hands in his pockets. "I knew he had to be hallucinating or something to think Claudia was cheating on him."

"Guess this is my fault. Well, John's fault. That's fine. It gives me another reason to yell at him."

"As long as you aren't yelling at me anymore."

"About that..." Beatriz began, tucking a strand of hair behind her ear in nervousness. "I'm sorry. I overreacted and—"

Ben held up his hand and Beatriz fell silent.

"You never asked me how I know Spanish," he said. "Ever been curious?"

"Not really," she admitted. "I assumed you learned it in high school."

"I didn't. How old were you in your senior year of college?" Ben asked.

"Twenty-one."

"Right. I was twenty-three. Ever wonder

why I was two years older than Henry our senior year?"

"I just assumed you'd been held back in high school," she teased.

Ben laughed. "Not quite. I graduated salutatorian. Brooks was my dream school but scholarships and student loans didn't cover the tuition. I got a job after high school. Construction work. And then I got a second job—waiting tables at a Mexican restaurant. I did both for two years before I could afford Brooks."

"I didn't know that," Beatriz said. "You fit in so well with Henry and Claudia that I thought you were one of them."

"Rich kids?"

"Right."

"I'm not. Never was. I worked my ass off to afford Brooks. My parents worked their asses off for me to afford Brooks. I didn't think they'd be thrilled to hear that I'd turned down the six-figure job waiting for me after college because I'd fallen for a freshman and needed to hang around a few years until she graduated."

"I wouldn't want to make that phone call either," Beatriz admitted.

Ben shrugged. "It's no big deal. Mom and

Dad never acted like they minded what they had to sacrifice. But I minded. So I decided I'd have no commitments. If things got too serious with a girl, I broke up with her. I had one close friend—Henry. Casual dating. Bea, I didn't even join a frat. Nothing serious for me except the job at the end of the tunnel."

"You and I didn't get serious. We went on one date. Not even a date. Half a date," she reminded him. One walk around campus, talking, and the kiss to end all kisses.

"No, but we would have," Ben said. "That was love at first sight, and I'm not even kidding. I couldn't believe how crazy I was about you. It scared the hell out of me."

"Why? I'm not that scary, I promise."

"You were then," Ben said. "You were a freshman. I was going to graduate. I had a great job already waiting for me on the other side of the country.... I was scared to death you were going to give me a reason to fuck all that up."

"Thanks for thinking I'd ruin your life."

Ben laughed and squeezed her knee. The heat from his hand seeped into her skin. She wanted to wrap her arms around Ben and hold him, but held back. He had to talk and she had to listen.

"It's not that. You couldn't ruin anyone's life if you tried. I just had my eyes forward and on the future, on what would happen as soon as I graduated. I didn't want anyone giving me a reason to look back."

"And I made you want to look back?" Beatriz asked.

"You," he said, taking her face in his hands, "made me want to look at you. Always. All the time. All day and all night. And so when Henry asked me to back off…"

"You backed off."

Ben nodded. "It was the perfect excuse. 'Do the right thing, Ben. Your best friend asks you not to sleep with his girlfriend's little sister, then you don't sleep with your best friend's girlfriend's little sister.' And I could pat myself on the back for being such a good friend. But the truth was, I probably would have slept with you and broken up with you like Henry said I would have. And not because I wasn't crazy about you, but because I was so crazy about you, it scared me."

"I'm going to try to take that as a compliment."

"It is. Bea…my father sold his Harley Davidson, which he'd saved up for since he was fifteen, to help me pay for Brooks. The most beautiful bike on the planet. He sold it without batting an eye. I couldn't pay him back by screwing up my future."

Beatriz smiled at him. "I like your dad. Sounds like a wonderful man."

"He is. Hope I take after him."

"I verbally castrated you today and you took it like a man, found Henry, saved their wedding, and didn't once tell me to shut the hell up."

"Well...your sexy Spanish accent comes out when you're mad. I should piss you off more often."

Beatriz laughed and ran a hand through her hair while trying to think of the best words to say to him. She found two words very quickly.

"I'm sorry."

Ben took her hand and kissed the back of it. "So am I."

"So now what?" she asked, squeezing his hand.

"We do need to get back to our work, don't we?" Ben asked and Beatriz raised her eyebrow at him. "What? Too soon?"

Beatriz burst into laughter and she stood up in front of him. She took his phone from his hand and laid it on the bedside table.

"Never too soon," she said and started undressing.

Ben stood up and ran his hands down her back before slipping them under her dress. He cupped her bottom and squeezed.

"So what chapter are we on?" Ben slid the straps of her dress down and pushed it all the way to the floor. They quickly dispensed with all her clothes and his, too.

"Anal," Beatriz said as she dragged Ben down to the bed and on top of her. He kissed her roughly as his hands roved all over her naked body. She lifted her hips in an invitation and Ben pushed his thumb and index finger into her, letting the knuckle of his thumb grind deep into her G-spot. As she moved her hips in rhythm with his hand, she reached out and grabbed *THE MANUAL* off the bedside table.

Ben took the book from her hand and tossed it across the room.

"What did you do that for?" Beatriz asked, shocked by his violence to the book.

"Because, I got this." Ben grinned down at her and Beatriz's body temperature shot up from the heat in the look alone.

"You did say you were bi in college," she said.

"For like a week. But trust me, it was an educational week. You want to do this?"

Beatriz raised her head and kissed him. As she kissed him she felt the stirrings of something deep and dangerous, something she thought she had killed and buried back in college. Love. Stupid, foolish, stubborn love. Ben had let her chew him out and then instead of pouting or fighting back, he'd gone out and saved the day. And although he'd walk away from her again at the end of the week, she let go and let herself love him. She'd survived loving him and losing him before. She'd survive it again.

"I want to do everything with you, Ben."

He grinned down at her. "Everything?"

"Absolutely."

"Good. Your sex toys nearly train-wrecked a wedding today. I think we should put them to better use."

"I love the way you think."

They kissed again, kissed until Beatriz couldn't stand it anymore. She had to have him inside her. Gently Ben pushed her onto her stomach and let her lay there relaxing while he gathered all the necessary supplies. He kissed Beatriz's back, up and down her spine, and she shivered from the gentle pleasure. The kissing continued as he flipped open the lube, poured it onto his fingertips, and started to work it inside her. She pulled her knees into her chest to open herself up further.

"You're amazing. You know that, right?" Ben asked as he started to work his wet fingers into her.

"Always nice to hear from a man with three fingers in your asshole."

"That's what I mean. You're so comfortable with yourself. Nothing scares you or freaks you out."

"I hate centipedes."

"Okay, other than centipedes. I just mean you're so free and open. I love that about you."

"Well, you're smart, hilarious, and you hunted Henry down like a dog and dragged him back to reality. I love all that about you."

Ben rolled a condom on and covered himself in lubricant. Slowly he started to push into her. "God, you're tight," he groaned.

"That was a good groan?" Beatriz asked.

"The best groan. I could live and die inside you." He pushed in deeper.

"And that..." she moaned the words. "I love that about you."

"What?" Ben pushed himself a few more inches into her.

"Your cock. I love your cock. Especially when it's in me."

"That's its favorite place to be, I promise." He sank into her, all the way, as Beatriz took slow, deep breaths. Her body welcomed his in further with each exhalation.

Carefully, Ben began to thrust into her—long, slow thrusts, both gentle and deep. Her muscles twitched and tightened around him.

"*Ay dios mío, que rico,*" she half breathed, half moaned.

"I only caught the first part of that," he said. "Oh, God, something something."

Beatriz turned her head to the side and he saw the smile on her face. "I said, 'Oh, God, that's good.' When I'm this turned on, I forget English."

"Good sign then. Let's see if I can get any more Spanish out of you." Ben picked up the dildo that had arrived for Beatriz under Claudia's name. Beatriz laughed a rich, throaty laugh. She'd forgotten the last time she'd been this turned on.

"I knew you were the right man for this job," she said as he knelt behind her again.

She shivered as Ben ran his hand up and down her naked back again.

"Beatriz...you should know, this might just be work for you, for your column, but it's not for me. I mean, for me, this isn't work. I hope that's okay."

She heard the sincerity in his voice, the hunger and the heat, and also something more. More than passion, more than lust. It penetrated her right to the heart.

"It's okay, Ben. It's more than work for me, too. A lot more."

"Good," he said softly and Beatriz swallowed hard and said nothing more. If she said anything it would be, "I'm falling in love with you again," and she wasn't ready to say that yet. So instead she spread her legs wider as Ben came up on his hands and knees behind her. What she couldn't say with her words she would say with her body. Ben pushed the dildo into her vagina. That was the easy part. Once more Ben started to enter her anally. He went even slower this time, which she appreciated. She wanted him inside her, filling her up completely, but she didn't want him to rush it.

"Is this too much?" he asked as he started to work his way into her again. With the dildo inside her, Beatriz felt even tighter.

"No. I love it. It's tight, and I feel really full, but in a good way. Don't stop."

"That's all I needed to hear."

Beatriz slipped a hand between her legs to hold the dildo in place so Ben could focus his entire attention on getting back inside her. It took longer this time. He pushed in an inch and stopped to let her adjust to him. Then another inch. In a few minutes she'd taken his full length inside her. She loved how careful he was with her, how controlled. Once he was fully penetrating her again, Ben eased them both down flat onto the bed and covered her hands with his.

As he moved in her, she studied the sight of his hands over her hands, their fingers twined together. She shouldn't feel this much, want him this much. She clung to his hand and wished she never had to let it go.

Ben kept his movements short and cautious as he pushed in and out of her.

"How does it feel?" she asked him. From his ragged breaths she could tell he was enjoying himself.

"Tight. Unbelievably tight. I could come any second now."

"You can if you need to," she offered.

"No way. That's the last thing I want. I want to be inside you as long as I can."

Ben kissed her back and shoulders as Beatriz writhed and panted underneath him, English and Spanish both lost to her now.

Ben reached around her hip and pressed two fingers on either side of her clitoris. She wanted to come so badly, wanted them to come together, something they hadn't achieved yet. Her soft moans grew louder, more desperate and hungry.

"Come with me," she said, her voice barely audible between breaths.

With his fingers working her clitoris, he thrust faster and harder into her. She'd never felt such pressure in her back and stomach. Every muscle in her body had gone taut as steel. Her ears buzzed as Ben's hips pumped against her and not even a gun to her head could have stopped the orgasm that exploded from her and into him. As she rode out her climax, she felt Ben stiffen on top of her before he groaned, grinding his own orgasm into her.

As soon as Beatriz came they both caught their breaths. Ben carefully pulled out of her. She grunted in some discomfort but then laughed at herself.

"We don't have any wedding stuff to do

today?" she asked as she rolled onto her back and opened her legs. Ben slid the dildo out of her.

"Nope. Why?

"I don't think I'll be able to walk until tomorrow. Or the next day. Maybe ever."

"Walking's overrated," Ben said before kissing her. "And I'm not letting you out of bed until tomorrow."

"What if I want to give you another blow job in the shower?"

Ben paused, clearly considering the question.

"Okay," he said. "Exception for blow jobs."

Beatriz stretched out on his chest and settled against him. She had never felt such contentment. This went beyond afterglow. Afterglow was a sunny day. She was walking on the surface of the sun itself. She wanted every night to be like this night. Sex or no sex she wanted to end every day with Ben. He made her laugh, made her come, made her smile even when he wasn't around. He'd failed her once and only once and she knew he would never do it again. He'd proven that today by finding Henry and saving the wedding. He was a good man, a beautiful man, the man she wanted in her life, in her bed and in her body.

Well, fuck her up the butt and call her Henry.

She was in love.

CHAPTER TWELVE

I t nearly gave the wedding planner a heart attack, but Claudia, five minutes before the wedding began, rearranged the order of the bridesmaids. She didn't care about height or symmetry. She only wanted to tease Ben and Beatriz by forcing them to walk down the aisle side-by-side at the end of the wedding.

Beatriz didn't complain at all about her new escort.

The music started and two ushers opened the double doors. In an elegant single file, the bridesmaids stepped onto the red-carpeted aisle in their matching orchid-hued dresses. Beatriz couldn't stop smiling as the music played and the guests turned their heads. Ben grinned back at her, the huge grin on his face rendering him so breathtakingly handsome she almost ran up the aisle. The past four days had passed in a blur of sex and laughter and more sex and trying to write her book review while Ben did everything he could to distract her. Typing with Ben's head between her legs was one of the most challenging and enjoyable writing experiences of her life. Especially since she had to balance the laptop against his forehead.

She took her spot on the opposite side from the groomsmen and tried to focus on the wedding. Claudia looked breathtaking in her strapless Vera Wang gown. Henry had already teared up and was trying not to show it. Beatriz half hoped Claudia would include in her vows a promise to never fuck Henry up the butt. Poor guy—he didn't know what he was missing.

Beatriz knew what she would be missing: Ben. Today was Saturday. Her flight and his flight left first thing tomorrow. She'd return to D.C., where she'd gotten a one-year contract working on a large translation project. Ben would go back to the West Coast, where he'd settled after college. She couldn't imagine how much she would miss him. And not just the sex, but him—everything about him. Between fucking sessions the past four days, they'd gone for walks together along the river's edge. They'd watched a movie together and had thrown popcorn at each other. They'd had long talks about what they'd been doing since college and what they wanted to do in the future. She admired Ben for not obsessing over climbing a corporate ladder. He only wanted enough money to own a nice place to live, travel, and enjoy his life. She talked about wanting to go back to El Salvador and reconnect with friends of her parents and relatives. He said if she didn't want to go alone, he'd go with her.

She didn't want to go alone. She wanted Ben with her now and always. She'd only planned for him to spend the week inside her body. Somehow he'd gotten inside her heart, as well.

A single tear ran down her face as Henry and Claudia kissed and the assembled guests burst into cheers and applause. They would have a beautiful life together. They'd already started talking about when they'd have children and the house they would be buying in the suburbs. Good for them. If anyone deserved happiness, it was Henry and Claudia. And Ben. Of course Ben. Maybe she could find a way to give him equal happiness—minus the suburbs.

She walked to the center of the aisle. Ben met her with his arm out. She took it and smiled up at him.

"I have something for you," she whispered between smiles at the guests.

"Does it come in a plain brown wrapper?"

"No. But I think you'll like it anyway."

She reached into the neckline of her dress and pulled out a folded piece of paper.

"What is it?" he asked.

"The review I wrote about the book."

He grinned, but didn't unfold the sheet.

"I sort of wrote something, too. But you don't have to use it on the blog," he said, digging into the pocket of his tuxedo jacket. "I hope you like it."

Once more they were separated as the crowd made its way out of the hotel ballroom and toward the restaurant that they'd reserved for the reception. Ben was led outside with the other groomsmen for a set of pictures. Claudia stayed with the other bridesmaids as they helped pin up her long train.

But Beatriz couldn't wait to read Ben's note. She excused herself, saying she needed something from her hotel room, and raced to the elevator.

Once inside her room, she opened the note.

THE MANUAL might be the greatest sex book ever written.

It might be the worst.

But I have to give it five stars or bees or whatever because it allowed me to have the best week of my life with the most amazing woman on Earth. This book should probably come with a warning— be careful, or you might just fall in love with your partner. I know I did. I love her and I want her in my life forever. And I never want to walk away from her naked, goddess-like body ever again.

Also, chapter six on woman-on-top positions was my favorite. Because boobs.

Beatriz slapped her hand over her mouth to silence her laugh. But it didn't work. The laugh bubbled up out of her. Her heart danced in her chest. She could barely breathe or stand.

"Ben loves me?" she asked the empty room. "Why?"

But then she decided she didn't care why. She just wanted to find him and kiss him and tell him the same thing.

Then again, she didn't have to.

Her review would.

CHAPTER THIRTEEN

Ben excused himself to go to the bathroom. It took ten minutes for the photographer to find the right light and angle for every stupid picture. Surely they wouldn't begrudge him a bathroom break. He nearly ran for it, wanting some privacy to read Beatriz's review. Since the review was going to be all about them having sex, reading it in a bathroom stall seemed the safest way to go. He locked the stall door, leaned back against it, opened the note and started reading.

Five big buzzing bees to *THE MANUAL*. Friends, Miss Bea loved this wonderfully witty and insightful sex position manual with the SHOUTY CAPS title. While other sex position manuals focus on the intimate details of the sexing and confuse readers with fancy terminology and complex position names, *THE MANUAL* simplifies things, throws in a sense of humor, and gives you enough information and encouragement to just do it.

And boy, did we do it. A lot.

My partner and I started with the modified missionary positions. Does your partner have an amazing body? Mine definitely does. This position allowed me to get a great look at it during sex. The Figure Eight brought us face-to-face. Does your partner kiss so well he makes your thighs melt? Mine does. Figure Eight was a win for that reason alone.

The tips on oral sex worked as well, although there isn't room for much improvisation in the art of the blow job. I appreciated the paragraph on how to modify your technique if your partner is well-endowed (like mine is).

The chapter on anal sex was especially helpful as it suggested trying double penetration using a toy. The position gave me the best orgasm of my life. And yes, Miss Bea keeps track of these things. I even have an orgasm spreadsheet.

The review continued. Beatriz had something nice and sexy to say about every chapter in the book. But it was the last paragraph that really got his attention.

As much as I enjoyed *THE MANUAL*, I do have to add one caveat. No sex position, no matter how well-written, can make up for the lack of a good partner. A good partner can make even awkward sex enjoyable. If the sex doesn't work, at least you can laugh about it together. A good partner makes sure you are enjoying yourself as much as he is enjoying himself. A good partner is adventurous, open-minded, willing to try anything his partner wants to try. I had such a partner this week and the only thing I can say is, Back off, ladies. He's mine. The only thing I loved more than the sex I had while trying out *THE MANUAL* is the man I had it with.

Sex, Love and Bees,

Miss Bea Haven

Ben stared at the last sentence and read it over and over and over again.

The only thing I loved more than the sex is the man I had it with.

Beatriz loved him?

"I have to love her back for the rest of my life," he said to himself. "It's the only gentle-manly thing to do."

Ben raced from the bathroom and ran to the restaurant. He glanced around for Beatriz, but didn't see her anywhere.

"Claudia, where's Bea?" he asked, interrupting her conversation without remorse.

"She said she had to run up to her hotel room for a second. What's wrong?"

"Nothing. It's just that I love her, and she loves me. It's an emergency."

"Love *is* an emergency. Go get her. Just hurry back. We've got cake."

Cake would have to wait. Ben headed to the elevators. If the elevator had broken the sound barrier getting to Beatriz's floor it wouldn't have been fast enough. At last he made it to her room. Before he could knock on the door, it flew open.

"Ben."

"Bea."

"I was just coming back down. To you. To

see you, I mean." Beatriz held up his note. "You love me?"

"Yes. Like crazy. You love me."

"That wasn't a question, was it?"

"No. I just like saying it." Ben took her in his arms and held her close. He'd walked away from her five years ago. Never again. "You love me."

"I do," Beatriz said. "I thought I was over you. But then I was under you. And now I'm in love with you. And it sucks because we both leave tomorrow."

Ben shook his head. "This isn't the 1800's. There are airplanes and trains and cars. Do you have to go back to work Monday?"

"I work from home most of the time."

"Then you can work from my home. Just change your flight."

Beatriz grinned. "I can do that. I will do that."

"Good. You do that. I'll do this." Ben kissed her hard on the lips and she opened her mouth to him. He pushed her back as he kissed her and pulled the silk ribbon from her hair.

"What are you doing?" Beatriz demanded, trying to sound stern, but laughing instead.

"This," he said and pushed her onto her back on the bed.

"Ben, we have to—"

"Nothing. We have to do nothing but this," Ben said and unzipped his tuxedo pants as Beatriz yanked the full skirt of her purple bridesmaid's dress up. Beatriz had on stockings and garters under her dress so he just grabbed the flimsy fabric of her panties and ripped them off. He didn't have time to negotiate with uncooperative lingerie. With the long silk ribbon he tied her wrists to the headboard.

"You're tying me up?"

"I don't want you getting away from me again."

"Have you been tested for everything?" Beatriz asked.

"Everything," he said. "Had a physical last month."

"I'm good, too. Clean and on birth control. Skip the condom?"

"Yes, please."

He pushed inside her as she wrapped her stockinged legs around his back. The raw heat of her around his bare penis made his eyes nearly water with the incredible shock of pleasure. He pounded into her like a madman and she took everything he gave her, raising her hips to meet his thrusts. He had to come in her, had to fill her with his semen, had to make her completely his.

The frenzied sex lasted only minutes. Beatriz came so hard her shoulders lifted off the bed and he felt her vaginal muscles slamming into his cock. He came seconds after, pouring into her as he thrust with everything he had.

He pulled out of her, still gasping, untied her hands, and passed her the box of tissues.

"Sorry about that," he said as she started wiping herself off.

"Don't worry. Claudia paid for the dress. A little cum never killed anyone."

"We should probably go back downstairs. Do I look like I just fucked someone's brains out?"

Beatriz stood up and pulled a new pair of panties on under her dress. "Yes."

"Good."

They returned to the reception, now in full swing. Both Henry and Claudia gave him the "we know what you've been doing" eyes. They tried to play it innocent. Ben justified his ravenous fucking of Beatriz by telling himself if he hadn't fucked her before the reception, he'd be sporting an erection during the entire rest of the evening. He was really doing the guests a favor by getting it out of his system.

He and Beatriz danced. Then he danced with Claudia while Beatriz danced with Henry. The night wore on and everything coalesced into a slightly inebriated haze of laughter, music, alcohol, dirty jokes, and cake.

And love. So much love.

At midnight the limo arrived to haul away Henry and Claudia to the tiny B and B where they'd planned to spend their wedding night before heading to Key West the next day. Beatriz helped Claudia with her dress. Ben helped Henry with his walking.

Just before the bride and groom shut the door, Claudia smiled up at them.

"We're re-gifting you a wedding present my weird cousin Griffin from New York sent us. It's not our thing, but I think you two might like it. I sent it up to your room, Bea."

And with that they closed the door and drove off.

Ben looked at Beatriz. "You think it's safe to get out of here?"

The reception seemed to be emptying out.

"Hell yes," she said and took his hand.

When they reached her hotel room, Beatriz found a white box sitting outside the door. They took it inside and laid it on the bed.

"I'm scared," she said.

"Me, too. Terrified."

"Should I open it?" Beatriz asked.

"If you don't, I will."

Beatriz lifted the lid off the beautifully wrapped box and pushed the tissue paper aside.

Ben leaned over and peeked inside. He raised an eyebrow at Beatriz.

"Well, we did finish *THE MANUAL*," she said. "And John did ask me to branch out into reviewing other kinds of sex toys."

"I'm game if you are."

Beatriz pulled a book out of the box. Underneath it lay a pair of handcuffs, some sort of whip, two floggers, and something that looked like a paddle made of leather instead of wood.

She threw a copy of *Kink for Beginners* onto the bed.

Ben glanced down at the book and back up at Beatriz.

"God, I love your job."

ABOUT THE AUTHOR

Tiffany Reisz is the *USA Today* bestselling author of the Romance Writers of America RITA®-winning Original Sinners series.

Her erotic fantasy *The Red*—the first entry in the Godwicks series, self-published under the banner 8th Circle Press—was named an NPR Best Book of the Year and a Goodreads Best Romance of the Month.

Tiffany lives in Kentucky with her husband, author Andrew Shaffer, and their two cats. The cats are not writers.

Subscribe to the *Tiffany Reisz email newsletter:*

www.tiffanyreisz.com/mailing-list

PULP
TIFFANY REISZ
THE ORIGINAL SINNERS
PULP LIBRARY
SAMPLER

Five of Mistress Nora's favorite client stories from Kingsley's files.

Previously released as two separate novellas, Immersed In Pleasure *and* Submit To Desire *are now available in one book.*

You're invited to Kingsley Edge's annual King's Trust Charity Auction.

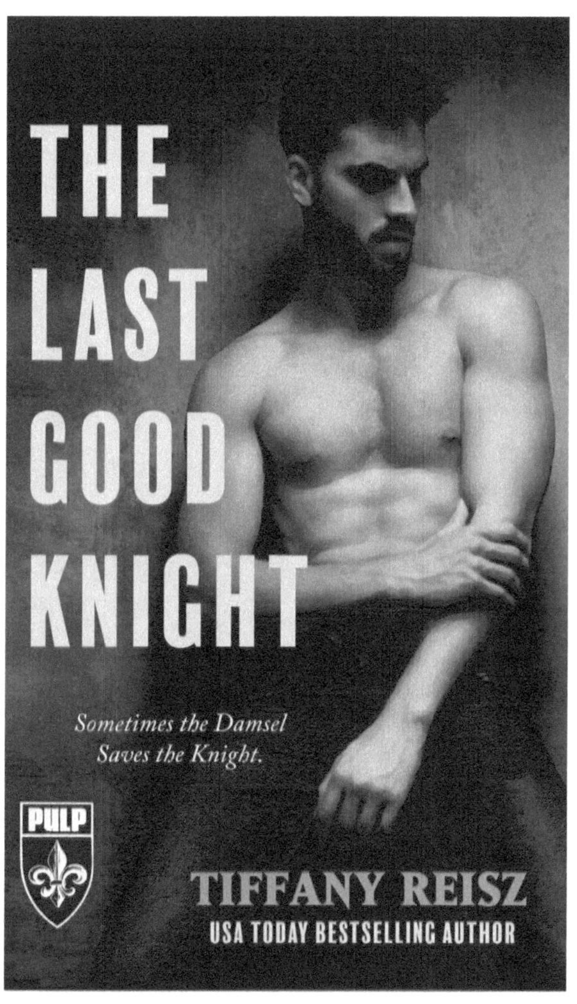

It's lust at first sight when Mistress Nora encounters Lance, a sexy newcomer to The 8th Circle.

A night of forbidden passion leads to a feud between two powerful horse-racing families.